USA TODAY BESTSELLING AUTHOR

DALE MAYER

contemporary
romance

SKIN

BROKEN BUT... MENDING #1

SKIN
Beverly Dale Mayer
Valley Publishing Ltd.

ISBN-13: 978-1-988315-87-4
Print Edition

About This Book

Forced to deal with very deep and individual problems, Kane and Tania – strangers who are complete opposites – agree to an assignment that includes only the two of them and that initially seems radical and a little scary.

Kane was ruthlessly betrayed by someone he trusted. The anger he can't seem to exorcise prevents him from grasping the only thing that can mend the damage: forgiveness.

Tania was raped, and her inability to deal with the trauma has kept her from the intimacy she nevertheless longs for in a romantic relationship. She's spent the years since the brutal attack she endured hiding behind her favored medium of expression. With her camera, she's kept the world at a distance, but the therapy requires her to step infinitely closer to her subject. As she immerses herself in Kane's skin – and his very male, physical body – Tania learns about beauty, compassion, strength, and wholeness.

Together, two broken souls take a journey of exploration, love, and ultimately healing.

Sign up to be notified of all Dale's releases here!
https://geni.us/DaleNews

CHAPTER 1

TANIA TOOK HER seat in the small room. She was early, and the seminar room was empty. She liked to arrive early in class because it gave her time to settle before things got started.

She'd been in similar scenarios before. She could do this, again and again, if she had to. Using the meditation tricks she learned, she practiced her deep-breathing techniques to ease back the stress threatening to choke the breath from her body. Therapy was good for her. She was getting better. She could do this.

This particular program was special, a university workshop type of thing. Intensive, invasive, and guaranteed to help bring about change.

She could do this.

Liar. She so sucked at this.

She stared out the large windows, her nerves raw, hot. Morning sunshine shone through the curtains, giving a muted look to the bright light. Kind of like her own life. As if she was living only a shade of the life she could be.

That was precisely what she was doing.

Several other attendees entered and took their seats. Special group, special problems, and they'd all signed up to do this willingly; had even paid for it. More than that, once committed there was no quitting. They were all students here at the University of British Columbia in Vancouver. They were all associated in one way or another with the professor who'd be leading this weeklong session. She was friends with one of the participants and recognized most of the others from Jenna's lectures on internal healing.

In her case, her best friend had paid the hefty deposit to hold Tania's place while she convinced her to get help. Five days in a hotel at the edge of campus. Workshops in the mornings, assignments in the afternoons, and therapy sessions dotted the rest of the evening. Even those who lived locally weren't allowed to leave at the end of the day; it was all-inclusive. She wished it were otherwise, then she could return to her normal life instead of this intensive, no-hiding type of session. Which was, of course, the purpose of the seminar.

She was scared, but she was more scared of staying caught in this limbo forever.

It was stupid. She shouldn't need help, not after all this time. It had happened years ago. She should be over this.

But the sad fact was, she wasn't. And if she didn't do something about it, her life would never go in the direction she wanted it to go. Her dream of a small house and white picket fence with the perfect two kids was never going to happen if she didn't find a way to let a man into her bedroom. *Sure,* she thought moodily, *I could adopt.* She had seriously considered it.

But she wanted the loving relationships she saw so many of her friends enjoying and to get there, she had to heal herself first. So not easy.

She smiled as her friend, Robin, came in and sat down beside her. Robin said, "Hi. How are you doing this week?"

Tania smiled wider. "Fine. As long as I avoid men, as

usual.”

"Ha." Robin grinned. "Defeats the purpose, doesn't it?"

"It's what I can do." Tania shrugged. "Leaving the safety net is not easy."

"I hear you." Robin settled in beside her. Tania's scars were inside, but Robin's were outside. She had been in a horrible accident and was dealing with reconstructive surgery and the fact she might never be 'normal'. She had trouble going out in public and had barricaded herself in a secular life of school. Robin was here to deal with her fears and how she looked now, and to find the strength to get out in public where she'd be ridiculed and stared at. After children had run from her screaming in a park almost a year ago, she'd gone home and stayed home. It had become the safe haven she didn't want to leave, but that also made it a prison. She had to force herself to go to class. Had to force herself to come to this seminar.

Tania understood.

They were all here to deal with issues – big issues. Whatever issues stopped them from living full lives. Their professor was a special woman who'd walked their path and had healed herself. Now, she was on a journey to help others do the same.

Just then, several men walked in, loud and boisterous. There was just something about that big, dominant energy as it filled the small, casual lounge. It was the same three men who arrived as a group last night. It was the same way they arrived at Jenna's classes on campus. Every week the quiet disappeared, and Tania and Robin became even quieter. This wasn't a normal therapy group – she'd been to those. This one demanded a commitment to complete the session and participation at all times. There was homework, assignments that forced participants to step out of their comfort zone.

Everyone knew something about each other, but the details had been offered at the discretion of the person. They were all here for a week. One week. Working together, pairing up for various assignments.

She *could* do this.

Then *he* walked in and sat down beside her.

Her stomach dropped and her blood heated. She could hardly breathe. She straightened and shifted ever so slightly closer to Robin like she always did. Like a moth to a flame, she knew better than to get any closer to Kane, a huge muscled guy who seemed too rough and…angry for her to be safe. But, just like the moth, the attraction was at the cellular level and she was helpless to resist.

God, she wanted him.

And she'd never wanted a man in her life.

He terrified her. She wanted to want a small man, someone her size. Someone…she'd have a chance to escape from if he turned abusive. Someone gentle, tender, and understanding.

Kane oozed strength, power, and bitterness.

Not at all what she wanted or needed.

Kane crossed his arms, his muscles bulging beside her. She shuddered. How could she want to stroke her fingers across his skin at the same time that she wanted to run away from him? He could pound her into the ground with one punch. Why? Why would her body want anything to do with him? It made no sense.

It only reinforced that she was crazy.

"Ah, Tania? Can you move back over slightly?" Robin gave her a concerned look then nudged her shoulder and, using her chin, pointed to Tania's half-empty seat.

Tania realized she'd damn near crawled into Robin's chair with her; she was that close. With a sideways glance at Kane, Tania flushed and settled back into place. "Sorry," she whispered to Robin.

"Don't worry about it."

Two voices said the same thing.

She wanted to yell 'snap', that silly remnant from her childhood, but was too busy staring in surprise at Kane. He gave her a stone-faced look. She'd never considered how her constant avoidance of him must look. He was no monster; in fact, he was stunning – to her. He had a lean face full of angles and planes. She thought of granite when she contemplated him. Strong. Infallible. Unyielding.

She had no basis for such an assessment. She didn't know him outside of seeing him once in a while in Jenna's classes. They were of a similar age, she thought, but he seemed older. It was his demeanor, slightly off-putting as he almost always had a sneer on his face. As if he was here under duress, but he didn't truly belong.

But then, she'd had a similar attitude in her last therapy class. That she didn't now meant she'd grown a little. Maybe he just needed a bit more time. Accepting one had a problem was a hell of a start – and often the most difficult step.

He might not want to see himself as one of the participants here who needed help, but that was what he was. And being here meant he had issues regardless of his attitude, so he was no better than she was.

But his attitude needed some adjusting if he was going to get any benefit from the class. And considering the money he'd dumped into this, he'd better.

She couldn't help but wonder at his story. He had a chip on his shoulder obviously, and there was a thin layer of bitterness just below the surface. She had to think relation-ships were involved. From what she'd seen, there were some pretty screwed-up people in the world, and those here for this session had taken a hit from some of the worst.

It had been good for her to come here and see she wasn't alone in dealing with her problems, or that her problems were by no means the worst. One of the men was young, like nineteen…maybe or possibly younger, considering the sparse bristles on his chin. He had a raunchy humor and dead eyes. Another, Sean, was tall and lanky and seemed seriously old on the inside. He both scared her and struck a deep cord of sympathy inside. His mother had horribly abused him for years before she finally OD'd on drugs, and he'd been left with a legacy of pain.

And like so many others here, he'd been working on his healing for years. He hoped this retreat would get rid of his last stumbling block.

Tania wasn't so sure it could be possible. That look in his eye…

She shuddered, grateful she'd come as far as she had.

Now if only she could kick this fear and go all the way. Yet another school idiom that made her want to chuckle. What was wrong with her? It was as if she had a delayed teenage-hood. Maybe she had. She certainly hadn't spent it dreaming over movie stars or giggling in groups waiting for the special guys to walk by.

The door opened, admitting Jenna Price, their professor and therapist. She was a mix of ruthless compassion and steely resolve. She was determined that everyone here get something useful from this session. They weren't randomly accepted into this workshop; there had been a long list, which grew even longer every term, apparently. Money hadn't been the only criteria. The problems you were dealing with had to be something she felt would work in a group setting and she could help you move past, and so the other participants could help you to deal with your issues, too. She wasn't about everyone getting along, more about how the interaction would work to benefit everyone involved.

Jenna walked to the empty chair, her hand wrapped around a large china mug with a lid. She was a tea drinker. Apparently, at any time and any place she could always be seen with the mug. She was a stately woman, anywhere from her late thirties to mid-forties. Tania had no idea – just that she appeared to be competent. Now if only she held that magical key to getting Tania's life back on track.

"Good morning." Jenna placed the mug on the floor beside her. "Last night was basic. Today, we are going to get into the nitty-gritty stuff, and you are going to hurt. It's hard dealing with the issues we don't want to look at. It's painful to step out of our padded cloud and deal honestly and openly with what needs to be dealt with." She cast her warm but determined gaze around the room. "Remember, none of you are here by accident. You came because you want to deal with something, and you want change for yourself. Today is Day 1. You will have changed by Day 5; I guarantee it." Her gaze landed on Tania and Robin, a slight softening warming her chocolate-brown eyes. "We'll be working together as a group all morning. But after lunch, you will be put into groups of two with your weeklong assignment."

Weeklong assignment? That was the first Tania had heard anything about it. As long as it was in pairs, she was probably okay. She could work with Robin. That would most likely suit both of them.

Taking a deep breath, Tania turned her attention back

to the morning's work.

A long time later, Jenna opened a folder she'd brought with her and handed out sheets of paper to everyone. "This is the outline of the assignment. You will be given all afternoon every day for the rest of the week to work on this, with my help if need be, but let's make no mistake here: the assignment is not a cerebral one. Each of you must deal with people, the public, and yourselves for this to work."

A small knot of dread formed in Tania's stomach as she comprehended how very difficult such an assignment could be. Poor Robin; she'd have the worst time with this. Already Tania's mind was wandering, looking for ways to make it easier on her, and came to a full stop. No. That was not the answer. She'd be enabling Robin. Better for her to deal with her issues than to have Tania automatically assume she couldn't do it.

Tania would have her hands full herself.

She accepted the sheet of paper from Robin and handed the last one over to the silent Kane. At least he'd lost the bored look. She studied his body language, noticing that he sat a little straighter and locked his jaw. He wasn't as comfortable as he was letting on.

Interesting. So control was important to him. She filed the tidbit away and turned her attention back to class. Jenna had been taking pairs of people off to one side and speaking with them privately. She watched as Robin and the abused young male walked out of the room together. Tania was surprised at the compassion on Robin's face and on Sean's. What was going on?

She turned her attention back to the paper in her hand. The project was intended to push her out of her comfort zone while being within the scope of what she needed to learn to do. Given the private nature of her problem, she really didn't want to have to do anything really uncomfortable. It would be embarrassing and potentially crippling. As another pair of attendees left the room, she realized Jenna was speaking to two more, leaving her and Kane.

Her insides twisted in on themselves. Please, let her be wrong. She wanted Robin as a partner, not Kane. Maybe this had nothing to do with the project. But God, it really felt like it did. The longer she sat there waiting for her turn, the harder her fingers clenched the paper in her lap and the tighter the steel band around her chest constricted. She stared almost blindly as her knuckles turned white and her chest struggled to relax enough to let air in.

Oh God!

If she had to be partners with a man, let it be with a small one. Not Kane. Please, not the six-foot-four, 240-pound man who looked like he belonged with his mitts wrapped around a jackhammer all day.

She had nothing against construction workers, but she so didn't want anything to do with Kane where her problems were concerned. She was looking for so much less of a man.

And her mind called her on it. *Liar. You so want to have something to do with him.*

She had to correct herself. *No, I want to be able to do something with him, but I'm not there yet.* She slid a sideways glance at his massive thighs encased in tight jeans as he sat relaxed in the chair beside her. *And,* she repeated, *I might never get there.*

Then it was her turn.

"Tania and Kane." Jenna walked over to them and tugged a chair forward so she sat in front, making a triangle of their positions. "Sorry for making you wait."

It was on the tip of Tania's tongue to say 'no problem', but she couldn't get the words out. Feeling like a mouse caught in a horrible sense of knowing it was about to get pounced on, she sat, frozen…and waited.

She knew her fate was as bad as the mouse when Jenna said, "Let's discuss your project."

Tania felt more than saw Kane glance her way, but she heard his comment clear enough. "Are you sure this is a good idea? Maybe Tania would do better with someone else."

His smooth-as-chocolate voice sent waves of want through her, but the actual meaning sent rods of steel down her back, making her straighten in outrage.

"I'll be fine," she snapped and widened her gaze as she understood she'd just agreed to work with him. Oh, shit. That damn stubborn temper of hers.

"Good. I think you'll do just fine. Besides, your partnership isn't a spur-of-the-moment decision. I've been working on these pairings since you both confirmed you'd be here, and I think you'll work perfectly together." She studied the papers in her hand for a moment, as if unconcerned at the reception of the other two.

Tania knew she had to be perceptive to the change in the air, the tension. She also had to assume the woman knew what she was about, except Tania had been to some crazy therapists who should have dealt with their own crap before trying to counsel others.

She didn't *think* Jenna fell into the same category.

But who could know?

Hunkering down in the chair, she tried to open her mind to the concept of a team project, actually managing to laugh at herself. It was just for a few days. *Like, how hard could this be?*

Then she listened in growing horror to Jenna's explanation.

When Jenna fell silent, Tania could only stare at her in shock.

Thankfully, Kane appeared to have a handle on this and blasted Jenna with her sentiments exactly. "You want us to what?"

He stood up and stormed around the room. "Are you nuts?"

Tania couldn't agree more.

With his hands out, he said, "Look, I'm here and willing to do the work to deal with my stuff, but you're putting Tania in danger."

She what? Tania straightened. "Excuse me? What kind of danger?" Because she wasn't up for any, not in any way. She wanted a safe, controlled project so she could open the door to her comfort zone and put her big toe in to test the water; that was it.

Danger? Hell no. She'd had more than enough when she'd been raped over twelve years ago.

She wasn't going to be in any kind of danger – ever again.

KANE HAD SAT through enough today. Watching Tania's tiny body shift away from him from the moment he'd sat down – hell, probably from the moment he walked into the room, he knew she had some big-time man issues. He didn't get man-hater vibes from her, but a tiny woman would be easy prey for the wrong man. Unless she was a black belt in something, she had no protection from a man's anger. That she was here in therapy, he'd bet his years of experience she'd been in an abusive relationship. She was a creampuff for any guy over sixteen. For someone like him, hell, no way could he be around her.

He felt like he'd be slamming a teacup against the wall if he said anything in a harsh tone.

She was way too delicate for this class, for him, and for this project. The damn shrink had this one wrong.

There was no way anyone with his anger issues, his hatred of his ex, should be around someone who he could break in half with two fingers.

As he realized Tania was nodding in emphatic agreement, a tiny part of him was sorry for it. In the old days, he'd have loved to have been the knight in shining armor and help her deal with whatever issues she had. He'd seen enough sad cases in his years in law enforcement that he had some idea of what she might have gone through. It could be something completely different...but his instincts said he was close. Damn close.

The shrink smiled at them both, with that damn compassionate warmth that made him wonder if she lived with sunshine and pussycats all her life to have given her outlook a rosy tinge. Because that wasn't the reality as he knew it.

She had to know about him. They all interviewed to come here. Every one of them had spoken to her privately about their issues, and then they'd all attended her lectures at the university alongside their regular classes. While he might not know all of Tania's issues, he knew Jenna did.

And still she'd paired them together. Wondering what she could possibly be thinking, he slowly sat back down.

And wondered why.

CHAPTER 2

TANIA WATCHED SILENTLY and a bit regretfully as Kane blew through his temper and back into calm. Her father used to do that: blow up, cool down, and then refuel for the next blow. Her mother had always loved to get him going. They'd fought like cats and dogs all the time, but it hadn't weakened their relationship. They'd argued, debated, and made up with the same passion. Because they blew up often, bad feelings and irritations didn't build up to the point where they caused damage. They shared what they felt all the time – good and bad. It hadn't been the easiest childhood, but she'd always known where she stood on any issue. Bottom line – they loved each other and her.

Even after their divorce, she'd never doubted it. They were still friends today.

Kane looked to be of similar ilk.

It made him a little easier to understand. Except, in this instance, she wished he'd blow a little harder, a little louder. And get them out of this.

"It's only a project," Jenna was saying in her smooth, what-could-you-possibly-be-worried-about tone of voice.

That terrified Tania. She'd been through too much therapy to believe that tone of voice. And from the looks of him, Kane hadn't been through enough. He appeared to be falling for Jenna's line of bullshit.

Tania wasn't so easily swayed. She leaned forward. "Jenna, you know our history. I'm not sure what Kane's issue is, but you know mine."

Jenna smiled warmly at her and waited for her to continue, expectancy on her face for a favorite student about to give the right answer. That should have been enough warning, but just in case Jenna really didn't get it… "Surely," Tania added, "I could work with Robin. I'd love that." She beamed with relief at the smile on Jenna's face. This would work. Tania had always managed to get things to work at university and at work. People were accommodating; no one wanted discord.

Then she saw the look in Jenna's eyes and recognized there was to be no easy exit from this one.

"Fine. How hard can this be?" Tania glared at Kane, who just raised an eyebrow at her. He flicked something off his thigh, but it was the mocking look that made her ask. "What?"

"Oh, nothing; just flicking away an irritating mosquito."

She shot him a narrow-eyed look before turning her back on him to glare at Jenna. "This is a really bad idea," she said in a dark tone.

But Jenna was laughing. "Maybe and maybe not. So let's go over what you are going to do."

That was when Tania understood she was getting a camera.

A smile broke free, relieved laughter rippling throughout the room. "Oh my God! You should have said something in the beginning." She laughed and laughed.

When she could stop the giggles, only the odd hiccupping laugh still escaping, she realized Jenna had a wry smile on her face. Kane wore a thundercloud.

"I'm glad this isn't quite as impossible as you'd first been afraid it was," Jenna said gently.

And that, of course, had been the crux of the issue. Settling down, Tania relaxed, realizing she'd let her fears completely override rational thought here.

She loved photography, and of course Jenna knew that. They'd discussed it several times. She wasn't sure why or how, or if the sensation was real or just another mirage she put up in her world to make something doable, but being behind a camera put distance between her and a situation. It gave her a buffer from the uncomfortable, the too-intense insights, and the world at large.

It gave her a sense of security and of safety.

Jenna was seriously bright to have done this. Relief let Tania sit down and let herself settle inside. She was safe. This wasn't going to be something super scary or super intimate. In fact, she had to wonder if it would do anything for her at all, but her mind immediately clutched at the straw offered and said she could deal with the other stuff later down the road, like in ten years' time.

"Okay. I'm really going to love this project." Her mind wandered to the camera gear she'd brought with her, wondering what to use first. It all depended on what they had to photograph. Then another tidbit fell into place. "That's why you told me to be sure to bring my camera gear, isn't it?"

"Yes, it is." Jenna nodded, but she didn't look at Tania. Instead, she kept her gaze on Kane.

Realizing she'd been awash in her own satisfaction and joy at what she would be doing, she'd put no thought to Kane's role in all of this. It wasn't as if she needed him to carry stuff. It was all lightweight, and she'd been packing her gear for a long time.

She frowned as she took in the hard gaze between Jenna and Kane, realizing she'd missed something.

"Uhm, what's going on?" She studied the tick on Kane's jaw and recognized that instead of a blow-up, he'd gone super quiet. In her dad's case, it meant he was seriously pissed. She winced. Kane was going to have a monster of a headache after this. Clenching his jaw, his neck was corded, and as her gaze slipped down his chest, she realized his fists were almost white at the knuckles.

"Jenna?" No one could miss the signals in the room right now. She cleared her throat and tried again. "Maybe you could tell me what Kane and I are going to photograph?"

Kane, his voice like silken steel, answered instead. "Go ahead, Jenna." His voice deepened dangerously. "Tell us."

Shit. Tania's gaze raced from the one so furious she couldn't believe he was holding back to Jenna, who sat calmly, returning his stare in apparent unconcern. But Jenna was no fool; everyone knew you didn't turn your back on a dangerous animal.

And right now Kane was one hell of a dangerous animal.

"Why don't you tell her, if you think you know," Jenna said smoothly.

"Kane?" Tania wanted this tension to break. Even tensile strength had a breaking point.

"It's not what you're going to photograph," he snapped. "It's who."

Tania didn't understand, but at the approving curl on Jenna's lips, she figured Kane just got the favorite student award.

"Who am I supposed to photograph?" she asked, bewildered.

"Me."

KANE CLOSED THE door to his room with a very controlled click. He stood stock-still and let the anger ripple through him. He didn't dare let loose or there'd be a hole in the door. He splayed his fingers wide with as much force as he could manage. When the tension finally drained, he relaxed slightly. Then he took several steps toward the bed, where he threw himself down on the cushy surface. He leaned his head back and groaned out loud.

"What the hell am I doing here?" He could blame his brother for this damn session, but that wasn't fair. Sure, Jerry had pushed and prodded to get Kane to sign up, and it had been a good idea initially. Sounded like just what he needed. He'd been nursing his grudge for far too long.

It was time to move on before he screwed up other relationships.

He groaned again, lifting both hands and scrubbing his face. He only had an hour's lunch break. Everyone had split immediately after their meetings with Jenna, taking off for their own silent spaces. He needed food, but he'd needed space and time to regroup more. He could do a stupid camera project with Tania.

So what if she took a picture of him? Big deal.

Then why was he damn near shaking? It's as if he was stressed to the max and if that was the case, why? He'd been fine first thing this morning. Fine since he'd arrived. He'd been disdainful as the process started. It gave him a bit of buffer in case he started to feel too involved, or they got too dangerously close to his own hurts.

It was easier to come to something like this if he kept

himself separate from the others. And of course, the thera-pist's purpose was to stop him. He didn't know when he'd started to feel a fine edge of anger or bitterness to put more distance between them, but it was somewhere around the time he noticed Tania flinching away from him. This morning, she'd damned near crawled into Robin's lap.

It made for a tough few hours when every time he shift-ed, he felt her respond like a scared rabbit. He'd wanted to reassure her he wasn't planning on hitting her or hitting on her, but he'd known that would have made it all worse.

It was too bad.

She was tiny, delicate-featured, and curvy. He hadn't been able to stop thinking about her. Then with every breath he took, he was intimately aware of her reaction – just as she was aware of his every action.

To have that level of awareness with someone, someone who was terrified of him, was just wrong. No, he hadn't gotten the impression she was terrified of him…she didn't know him. He was a stranger to her. It was more she was terrified of what he represented.

His mind played with that.

What did he represent? Maleness. Strength. Power. He'd caught her gaze on his biceps. His thighs. He studied his arms; he kept in shape, worked out, and had a stocky build. No one would ever call him a toothpick.

From any other woman, he'd take her glances as interest. There could be a touch of that here, but he knew it wasn't the main part. Given they were in therapy, chances were good she'd been beaten up by someone bigger and stronger than her and most likely someone like himself – male.

It made it tough to sit beside her.

Because he didn't have the same issues. At least not over

sex. He *was* interested. Then again, he was male, so of course he was interested.

He grinned, his good humor restored. It would be a cold day in Hell before any healthy male wasn't interested in Tinkerbelle.

But to put the two of them together for hours on end was just asking for trouble. He wasn't sure he could stay calm and cool around her like she needed him to be, and he didn't want to terrorize her by blowing up in front of her.

She didn't need that.

He just didn't know what she did need, and it was none of his business. Jenna would have to sort that out. He needed to tell her privately to forget about this project.

Feeling better, he hopped up to his feet, prepared to go down to the restaurant for a quick bite, when it hit him. He was making a big deal over nothing.

This was a class project, just a few hours when he had to be in control, calm, and detached. Even cop-like would work. He was a cop. He was just back in school finishing his degree so he could move up the ranks.

She could take a few pictures, he'd learn a little patience, and he could go home.

Feeling better, he ran down the stairs, hoping to get a bite to eat after all.

Surprisingly, his appetite had returned.

CHAPTER 3

WHILE WORKING HER way through her lunch, Tania realized it was stupid to feel so relieved. She was here to face the parts of her she'd been keeping locked away. Finding out she got to hide behind the lens of a camera made this an easier assignment than she expected.

That Kane was going to be her subject filled her with mixed feelings. She adored playing with light and dark. The camera would love him; his muscles, that build. So much about him excited her to be able to do this.

And with the camera, she didn't feel in danger. He was no threat to her. She'd be able to keep a lens between them.

She knew photography. She understood images.

But she didn't know him. But she *would* know him by the time this assignment was over. There was no way she couldn't. Photography was a tool to study something. To learn about something she hadn't been able to access before. The lens brought her closer, highlighted the focus, and forced everything to drop away yet lifted the subject for closer inspection. It was almost as if he was standing naked. Alone, Vulnerable. Reachable.

She laid the fork back down beside her plate and stared off in the distance. Was it coincidental? Or had Jenna understood this could help Tania in a big way?

"Something wrong?" Robin asked across from her.

Tania shook her head. "Not really, just thinking about the assignments."

"Oh. Those." Robin sighed heavily. "Yeah, so not sure about that."

Part of the assignment instructions had been to keep the assignments private from the rest of the group so as not to be influenced by anyone else's thinking.

Robin attacked her fries with more force than necessary. She'd sat where her scarred face would be out of the public eye. The restaurant rumbled in a nice enough way to say it was busy but lacked the overpowering-noise element of being bustling.

It suited Tania fine. She could be lost in her own thoughts without anyone noticing.

Then Kane walked in. No, Kane didn't walk anywhere. He strode in, determined, loose-gaited, and ready for anything. Her photographer instincts kicked in. Kane definitely had presence. She could imagine screen producers loving him. He didn't just take over a space; he owned it.

Her fingers itched to run to her room for her camera.

Her hands actually clenched the table to hold herself back. With an inward shudder, she dragged her gaze away and caught Robin's wide-eyed stare.

She flushed as heat raced up her cheeks. "Sorry," she muttered.

"Oh, don't be. I would love an explanation though." Robin looked at her expectantly.

Tania shook her head. "Wish I could. It's part of the assignment we're doing."

"Uh-huh." Robin snorted lightly and dove back into her french fries. "Must be one hell of an assignment."

The teasing tone made Tania's cheeks heat up again. She

stuffed her mouth with salad so as to not have to answer. Lunch finished quickly. By the time they made their way back to the seminar room, Jenna was already getting the first groups started.

When it was Tania's turn, Jenna said, "Kane is going to maintain what would be his usual routine for the afternoon. This is where you will start. You need to come up with a title, a theme, and a series you can explain to me – if an explanation is necessary – of what and why and how."

Kane snorted. Tania spun around in surprise. She hadn't heard him come in. She frowned up at him, and he stared back, one eyebrow raised.

She wanted to ask what the hell he'd be doing for his half of this assignment besides lazing around all afternoon while she worked but held back. She had to trust that Jenna, who knew why Kane was here, had plans that would help him, too.

"We'll check back here at four. If you need any help, you can text or call me. I'll be in the morning room working." Jenna gave them a bright smile and walked away.

Damn.

Kane never said a word. Actually, she rarely heard him speak at all. She cleared her throat and said, "I have to get my camera from my room. What are you going to do?"

He stared at her then looked around. "If I were at home, I would be doing yard work. Here at a hotel, I might do a bit of sightseeing, watch a movie, go to the gym…"

"And your choice right now?"

He ran his fingers through his short, wavy hair and sighed. "I think I'd like to get the hell out. So a walk around the university sounds about right."

She brightened. "I love the university grounds. Perfect.

I'll go get my camera and meet you in the lobby." She took off.

KANE WATCHED HER run away. She was brighter, happier than he'd seen her yet. How bad could wasting a few hours pretending to be a tourist be? Especially with Tinkerbelle at his side?

He had no idea how this assignment was going to help him.

As he turned to stare at the empty room, he recognized Jenna standing off to the side watching him, waiting, as if she knew.

What the hell was he doing here? He looked at her. "How does being a model help me?" The derision in his voice brought a smile to her face, which was not quite the reaction he was hoping for.

"I think it's going to help a lot, actually." The serious tone surprised him.

"So me going out and being a tourist is going to help me deal with my anger issues?" He shook his head and started to walk away in disgust. "What a waste of time."

"Really? Except look at where your anger issues sprang from."

He stalled and leaned his head back to stare at the ceiling. "I prefer to *not* think about that time of my life, thank you."

"And that's why the anger. You need to examine it. The pain is more painful because you keep it alive…whereas the anger is a blind…for something else." She paused then added gently, "Maybe for fear."

He spun around, feeling the familiar anger vibrating

through his system. He glared at her. "I have to keep it alive, or else I will forget."

"No," she said, her voice gentle but determined. "You need to understand you are keeping the anger as justification for not letting anyone else get close. Never again."

He stared at her, hating the resonating truth to her words. "Easier said than done," he muttered.

"Not easy. None of this is easy. But for a full life you can enjoy again, it's necessary."

"And playing the tourist is going to do that?"

"Interesting you chose being a tourist. Casual. Distant. Disconnected."

He reared back. "What? You said to do what you would normally do. I can hardly go mow the lawn now, can I?"

Those all-too-knowing eyes studied him. He wanted to squirm and held himself strong against it. He was no schoolboy.

"There are other activities you could choose, and you don't have to play tourist all afternoon."

She reached out and patted him on the shoulder "You'll figure it out." And she walked away, leaving him wondering what the hell she was up to.

He pulled out his phone and texted his brother. *Waste of time and money.*

As he closed his phone, an overly bright, I'm-determined-to-do-this voice called out to him, "Are you ready?"

Knowing she couldn't see him, he rolled his eyes and turned around to face her. He could only hope she wasn't going to be wearing half-dozen cameras around her neck, or they'd really look like a pair of damn tourists.

Instead, she had a single black fanny pouch on her tiny

waist and a single camera around her neck. He knew nothing about cameras, but it didn't look to be a cheap, casual deal. She just might be a serious photographer, and for some reason, that made him feel better. He didn't know what she did for a living or what her education program was. He'd never seen her on campus except at Jenna's lectures. Still, she put her money into good equipment, and he could respect that.

If he had to play the gallant knight for a couple of days, whatever. And if a part of him wanted to give the no-refund policy of the damn contract a closer look, he pushed it to the back of his mind. What Jenna asked was impossible, but his pain didn't have to dim whatever problem Tinkerbelle was working on. He'd always been good at playing the stoic role. He could do this.

He nodded. "Let's go."

CHAPTER 4

TANIA UNDERSTOOD THE camera, just not the subject. Kane was difficult; a man of secrets. Getting him to be natural was the key. He was doing the posing-tourist role, and she wanted nothing to do with it. Still, it would take some time to find the real him inside.

She let him walk ahead on the cobblestone. There were intricate patterns worked into the street, and her camera loved them. Whenever he looked away or something caught Kane's eye, she tried to capture him.

But she didn't like the results. She'd have to ditch most of them at this rate.

"Coffee?" he asked hopefully, pointing to a small bistro off to the side.

"Tea?" she suggested, not knowing what they'd talk about.

He shrugged and led the way over. "I'll go in and order."

Happy to let him take charge, she nodded and took pictures of him walking into the tiny shop. He had a hell of a butt. What she wouldn't do to get him in tight boxers. The magic her camera could work then… Her thought was immediately followed by shock. Had she really just thought that? About a perfect stranger?

He returned in a few minutes with two mugs. "Hope this is okay. Black tea and black coffee."

She fished the tea bag out quickly, not wanting to have it too strong if there wasn't milk and not wanting to go in and get milk even if it was available. For a therapy seminar, so far she'd cried no tears and had yet to feel under the gun with questions or swamped by emotions. She felt odd, not herself. Normally, she'd have just asked him to get the tea the way she liked it, but not this time.

Was it doing any good?

As if reading her thoughts, Kane said, "Weirdest therapy session I've ever done."

She laughed. "Exactly what I was thinking. I feel like this assignment is supposed to do something, but we are completely missing the mark."

"Are we?" Moodily, he stared into the deepest, blackest mug of coffee she'd ever seen. "Seems like a complete waste of time so far."

She leaned forward. "That's what I mean. We're out here sightseeing when we should be working on healing."

He leaned back at her emphatic comment. "You think we shouldn't be out here."

She shrugged and looked around. "I can't help but feel like we are deliberately avoiding something. Or aren't ready yet to get too close to the real issues."

"Really?" he snorted. "What real issues? I highly doubt you want to share your issues with me. And I know I'm not going to. So what else are we supposed to be doing here?"

She stared at him, realizing she *could* share, but she didn't want to. And he was right; if they weren't going to help each other, what was the point? Unless one of them could help the other, and maybe in the helping, the other could be healed a little as well.

"Did you research Jenna's seminar?" She smiled at his

emphatic nod.

"Hell yes."

"And read the comments, reviews people had left?" When he nodded again, she said, "And do you recognize our conversation is similar to many that were written on her website? And I quote, 'I started the journey expecting to find the opposite of what I got. Thank God.' Or 'When I first started this seminar, I thought I'd signed up for the wrong one. It was nothing like what I'd expected.'"

He stared at her then leaned back, dropping his gaze to his cup. Speaking slowly, he said, "The one that resonated with me was, 'I don't understand the how or the why or the process that happened, but healing has started…'"

"Oh, I like that." Contemplative, she stared around as the traffic picked up slightly as more people came looking for sustenance. "I'm supposed to find a journey with you as my subject. I don't understand really, but I'm willing to trust a little here. Outside, it feels like it's an impersonal journey." She stopped and frowned. "I'm not really sure where I'm going with this, but say we were at home and you had the week off – what would you be doing?"

"Refinishing my bathroom."

The answer came so fast it surprised her.

He grinned with real humor, and his face came alive. She stared, entranced, as he spoke. "It's been the plan for a while. Now if you were to say, if I had a couple days off, what I would be doing, I guess I'd be working out, catching up on yard work, lazing around the house, and watching some classic movies."

As his mouth moved, her eyes caught on the lean muscles that formed and reformed in perfect symmetry. He was lean and hard and spoke about a world she didn't understand. And she was suddenly afraid she just might know what Jenna had been thinking.

And hoped not.

She raised her gaze to Kane's and watched light play across his features as his eyes darkened. He leaned closer, his whole body language shifting, softening. Damn, she wanted to photograph him.

"What's up, Tinkerbelle?"

That startled a laugh out of her. "Tinkerbelle?"

He waved an arm at her. "You're tiny, delicate, and look like a good wind would blow you away." He shrugged. "It just came to me."

And something just came to me, she thought. Sending up a prayer that she had this right and Kane wouldn't find her off the wall, she said, "I know this might sound a bit weird, but…" she took a deep breath, and then added, "You have a very photogenic face." She motioned to his biceps. They bulged and relaxed almost as if he was bunching to a tune in his mind. "In fact, your muscles are really interesting." As his eyebrows shot up to his hairline, she quickly corrected, "For the camera, I mean."

She looked away for a moment before forcing herself back on target. "I guess what I meant to say is that skin and muscles, how people move, have always fascinated me. If you are okay with it," she took a deep breath before she dropped her gaze to the table, wishing it were wider, deeper, higher – anything to increase that barrier – and said in a rush, the words tripping over themselves before she could take them back, "I'd like to take pictures as you work out."

Her shoulders and chest collapsed, completely empty. There, she'd done it, and he hadn't laughed yet. She peeked at him from under her lashes to see him still staring at her.

Shock turned to consideration, then to contemplation. She watched him throw down the napkin clenched in his fists. "Sure. Whatever."

Whatever? Did that mean he didn't mind? Or he was okay with her off-the-wall request? Or that he'd do anything to get through this assignment so he could go home? And did any of his reasons matter?

He did need to be comfortable with her doing this, or else it wouldn't work. The camera would pick up every nuance of his moods, his emotions. That was the thing about the images. They didn't lie.

Raw footage caught the truth. Sometimes more truth than anyone cared to have revealed. "I wouldn't want to make you uncomfortable, so if it's not okay, I'd rather hear the truth now."

He was watching the coffee swirl in his mug. After a moment, he raised his gaze to hers. There was a blind over his feelings, a sense of detached mockery coming through. She winced. "Okay, so it's not a good idea. Forget I mentioned it."

"No." He reached out to stop her as she'd instinctively pushed her chair back. "Wait."

She stilled as the heat of his hand soaked into her chilled skin, and she slowly sat back down. "I'm not trying to push your boundaries. I just thought this would be something I could do that would be within the parameters of the assignment and be something I would like to do. But I don't want to make you do something you don't want to do."

"And you can't." The corner of his mouth lifted. "But isn't doing what we're uncomfortable doing part of why we're here?"

"True."

"Are you taking an easy way out by doing something like this?" he asked. "Where's the uncomfortable part in all this for you if you want to do it?"

"I don't know. I hadn't actually realized I'd enjoy documenting the process until I recognized how much my eye was caught by your muscles." She reached out and laid her finger on the cord, tightening and relaxing on the back of his hand as he tapped the top of the table. "You're very mobile. I mean muscles shift, skin moves, light plays over all of you in different ways." She gave herself a mental nudge to pull back.

She was fascinated by what she was seeing, and she desperately wanted to do this project now she had a topic she could hold on to. She hated to admit it, but there was a solid chance she needed to do this. Maybe Jenna was right. "But it's your body, and it's your personal space. I didn't mean to intrude." That she had was already incredible. She was normally the mouse at the door waiting to run at the first hint of discord. Instead, here she was actually asking this super-male physique to do something he didn't likely want to do.

"It's a stupid idea," she said suddenly. "Forget it."

"No, I won't forget it." He motioned to her tea. "Settle down and drink your tea while I mull it over."

She picked up her cup and waited impatiently.

KANE STUDIED THE disgruntled look on Tania's face. Tinkerbelle had a temper. Well, so did he. She'd seen him blow at Jenna earlier, but that had merely been a trickle of what it could be. Still, she hadn't seemed phased by it. He'd half-expected her to have run from the room screaming, but instead, she'd sat there with a grin on her face.

Someone around her had a temper for her to be so blasé. Interesting.

Now, did he have a problem with her taking pictures while he lifted weights? He couldn't think of a decent reason to stop her, especially when she'd lit up at the idea like she'd been covered in fairy dust. He hadn't ever been photographed working out. It was hot, hard, and sweaty work. He didn't go to the gym to look for girls. He went with a trainer for some serious, anger-releasing work until he was dead-tired from the workouts, and there was nothing pretty about that.

He stared morosely into his empty mug. There was nothing pretty about any of this bullshit. As much as he couldn't say he was comfortable with the concept, he'd had a few friends who had participated in similar photo shoots, so it was more his comfort level at question here.

"As long as you don't post these pictures online and they are only for the project, then I am good with it." He looked up to stare into her eyes. "That goes for all the pictures you're taking. I'm the model, but I'm not giving you the rights to the images beyond the scope of this class."

She smiled, and the relief in her eyes was obvious.

She said, "I won't. These pictures are just for the project, and if there are one or two I really like, I'll ask you for permission if there is anything I want to use them for." She laughed. "What am I talking about? I don't do anything with my photography. I don't post them online at all." She pursed her lips. "Maybe it's something I should consider."

"I'm surprised you haven't. You appear to be serious about it."

Her hand instinctively went to the camera around her neck. "It's just a hobby, something to keep my mind and hands active."

He stood up. "Kind of like my workouts. Come on, let's hit the gym at the hotel. You can take pictures, and I can work on some of this restlessness."

She bounced to her feet and dashed ahead of him.

Eager much? Still, there were worse things in life than having a beautiful woman sit there and watch him lift weights.

CHAPTER 5

NSIDE THE HOTEL lobby, Tania stopped her headlong rush. Belatedly, she realized how it must have looked. She'd raced back to the hotel as he'd strolled behind her. She turned her head to see him just now approaching the front doors. How idiotic.

On the other hand, she couldn't remember the last time she'd been this excited. And it was photography related the last time, too. Too bad she couldn't make a living that way.

Working part time with preschool children had brought her from the dark ages into the light. The laughter and light of the little children reminded her of the good things in life, the joys in the mundane, the reason for living.

It also reminded her why she was here. So she could heal to the point of having a relationship and having children of her own. Just the thought of those tiny chubby arms wrapped around her neck and snuggling close brought tears to her eyes.

Kane moved past her toward the elevator. When she didn't fall into step behind him, he turned and asked, "Have you changed your mind?"

"No."

"Then come on. I have to get changed, and the gym is on a different floor."

She ran into the elevator behind him, hating how stupid

she must have looked. Of course, the fitness room was on a different floor, as were the other amenities. She stayed quiet until the door opened, then followed him into the hallway. He unlocked his room and pushed it open. She leaned back against the hallway and said, "I'll wait for you here."

"You can come in. I won't be a moment." He motioned for her to enter.

It felt stupid, but for some reason, her feet were obeying her mind and not her heart. She entered a man's bedroom for the first time in her life. Sure, it was a hotel bedroom, but it still counted…

"I'll get a few things."

And he disappeared from view, which gave her a chance to look around. Essentially, it was the same as her room, but slightly larger. There was a similar layout and look to the two rooms, but that was where the differences lay. His room had a suitcase and a large gym bag open on the bed, a few casual pieces of clothing lying around. He rummaged in the gym bag and pulled out a few things, including what looked like a pair of gloves that startled her, then an outfit. "Back in a moment." And he disappeared into the bathroom. She sat down on the edge of the single spare seat and lifted her camera to look through the lens.

Immediately, she felt better. The slight distance eased the discomfort of a new and uncomfortable situation. Inside, she was exultant. If only her friend, Jillian, could see her now. In fact, she'd take a few photos as proof. Quickly, she snapped a couple of shots of the male domain before he returned.

When the door opened, she'd retaken her seat and was making adjustments to the zoom. Looking around, she caught sight of him.

Her breath caught in her throat. Muscle shirts had been designed for men like him. Holy Hannah.

And she might be afraid of having sex, but apparently there was nothing wrong with her libido. His pants clung to his massive thighs and as he walked past her, she barely restrained her hand from reaching out and grabbing his ass to see if it was as rock-hard as it appeared. She shuddered.

He was to die for.

He pulled open the door, sighed, turned back her way, and said, "Are you coming?"

Heat swept through her. Her mind screamed, *I wish!* Her mouth mumbled, "Sorry. Lost in my thoughts."

"Whatever."

She scooted past him, careful not to touch him.

He shook his head slightly and locked the door behind her. "This way."

She followed along, lost in the rosy haze of lust, and wondered how people survived days of this. She'd never been one to moan over men in any size or shape, and now all she wanted to do was crawl up his frame.

Except, as soon as she touched him or he touched her, the situation would all change. There was no way it wouldn't.

And that was a sobering thought.

Cooler and more composed, she walked beside him, happy when he chose to take the stairs. He ran down lightly and she followed. She was in good shape, but she wasn't fit as in *fit* fit. She didn't work out, and she didn't do any crazy spin classes. She walked a lot and did yoga for stress relief. For some reason, twisting her body into crazy-ass positions always loosened her muscles. Probably because she stretched them past the point they'd normally go, so when she finally released them, they were like rubber and sagged in relief.

He pushed open the door to a lower level and led the way inside. It was a small but perfectly acceptable space as far as she was concerned. From the disgusted look on his, she figured the amenities were not up to his standards. Then again, a heavy fitness enthusiast probably needed more than the bits and pieces of equipment here. For her, it was fine. There were a few decent-sized mats leaning on one corner. She wouldn't mind doing a few yoga poses while she was here. She glanced down at her sandals and Capri pants. Not good. She wouldn't be able to maneuver in these clothes. Why hadn't she thought to get changed herself?

Stepping back to give him room, she watched him open the bag he'd brought down with him. There was a tub of chalk in the bag, and with a cloud of dust in the air, he pulled on his gloves.

He started with a few simple stretches to loosen up. She used the time to walk the room and change her settings for the interior light. There were no natural windows, and from the number of stairs they'd walked down, she had to assume they were below ground level. In spite of its location, the room was bright and open and boasted a full wall of mirrors. She took several pictures and adjusted the settings again. She shifted to a different lens, was unhappy with the results, and switched to another one. Finally satisfied, she turned back to Kane, watching as he performed a series of sit-ups, followed by pushups before locking into a nice, steady plank.

She might not work out, but she could certainly appreciate the ease and smoothness by which he switched from exercise to exercise. By the time she walked back over, she could see a thin shimmer of sweat on his skin. She immediately lifted her camera and clicked – then again and again.

She was lost as she tried to zoom in and capture that sheen to his skin, the effervescent glow that made his muscles shine. She shifted around him, moving carefully as he worked just as hard at what he was doing.

She hoped she wasn't disturbing him. He was a serious machine in motion. His gaze was inward, as if working on controlling his breathing and counting his movements. His muscles shifted and rippled as they answered his demands.

And boy, was he demanding.

He was doing different reps of different intensities in the floor-exercise portion. She almost laughed. She was good at sitting down and doing reps of eating cupcakes just as seriously. This man was definitely working out!

She was lost in bemusement as he crunched and lifted and flipped and did it all over again. She was exhausted just watching him.

Then she watched a bead of sweat roll down his forehead, and she went into action. She stared from where she stood and zoomed in as many stages as she could go, trying to capture that single drop as it stood poised on the pulsating cords lifted along his temple. Then it dropped.

She couldn't stop. She moved as close as she dared, clicking away as his jaw twitched and clenched and that chin firmed and the cheekbone locked down.

"He's something," she murmured to herself.

Then realized he'd stopped and was staring at her.

She lowered the camera, tilted her head slightly, and asked, "Is there a problem?"

He stared at her as if she'd asked a seriously stupid question, then shook his head and silently went back to work.

She was left wondering what she'd done, or what he'd thought she'd done.

REALLY? SHE THOUGHT he was something. That was intriguing. Tinkerbelle just might be interested. Except he wasn't sure she even knew what she was doing. She certainly hadn't appeared to recognize that she'd spoken her thought out loud. Most women he knew would never be so honest.

And he suspected she hadn't meant to be.

Sure, she was comfortable around a camera, but he had to wonder if she'd ever been around a man – not a boy but a full-grown, adult male – because she certainly wasn't acting like it. For someone her age, she appeared damn innocent.

At first, he'd managed to block her out as he got into the swing of it. He loved setting a rhythm and working his body through the paces. It felt good. It felt natural. It felt right.

And he managed to get through most of his warm-up until she fixated on his face. What the hell was she doing? She'd been quiet, taking the odd picture before she had suddenly gone click-happy, her fingers moving at a speed he could only guess at. Then she'd moved closer, and he understood she'd locked onto his face. And she appeared to be studying his forehead. It completely disconcerted him when he realized a drop of sweat had fallen from his brow to the padded floor and she dove after it to take a picture.

What was that about?

Why would she even think to focus on such a thing? He always worked up a sweat. Had she been taking pictures of his shirt as it slowly soaked up, too? He wanted to make a sarcastic remark then figured he better not bring attention to it – just in case she hadn't seen it yet.

He couldn't imagine what interest any of this would have for her, but she appeared enthralled. He closed his eyes and pushed his body through several more reps. The whirling click quickly became background noise. Then he stopped and rested. His body thrummed with energy, and fatigue had hit the muscles – that was a good thing. He stretched his arms up over his head and sighed gently.

"Feel good?" Her voice held an odd note. If he didn't know better, he'd say she was sending out mixed signals. He also couldn't get rid of the feeling that she had no idea what she was projecting. Or what she thought she was projecting.

She was like Tinkerbelle in the innocence department, too. He had to wonder if she could be, but her age and university status made it hard to believe. She wasn't model beautiful, but those huge, haunted eyes were enough to bring any man to his knees. It certainly brought out his protective instincts.

Another guy could easily use her as a punching bag. He'd assumed from her original trepidation around him that that had been her problem, but the camera had completely changed her.

It fascinated him.

He also assumed it was a surface change only, and that if he made a move on her, she'd bolt like lightning in the opposite direction.

There was a part of him really wanting to push the issue, too. Make her fess up to being as terrified as she really was. He knew it would be a shitty thing to do. He really wasn't that kind of guy, unless he was fucking pissed.

Then everyone was that kind of guy.

CHAPTER 6

SHE UNDERSTOOD SHE'D done something off, but for the first time in a long time, she was able to brush it away. She was doing something she loved with a subject that was fascinating. Even better, this activity was encouraged, necessary even.

A part of her wanted to squeal with joy. She'd wanted to take pictures of people for a long time, but there were rules and regulations and laws and…of course who she'd been interested in taking photos of versus the ones who were willing weren't the same, either.

Kane fascinated her.

And he was male. In the beginning – *was that only last night?* – he'd been imposing, scary, and forceful. She knew he could break her in two within seconds. She'd done a mess of self-defense courses and she'd have an edge if he tried anything, but there was no doubt that strength won out.

She'd spent the better part of the day capturing who he was, and although those fingers clenched into fists and his jaw clenched into stone, there was an element of control to him. As if he was afraid he'd cross the line…one day…but hadn't yet.

Not for the first time, she wondered at his story. Curiosity ate at her, but she didn't dare ask. Everyone struggled with personal boundaries in therapy. Some stories were meant to be told, others were told in parts, and even more would never see the light of day.

Hers was in the middle category. They used to be at the end. Progress.

In Kane's case, he was a cop back in university to finish his degree so he could move up and do more. There was an awareness, an alertness to everything going on around him at all times, as if he never rested. Never relaxed his guard. When they were at the coffee shop, there'd been a softening in his gaze a few times. She tried to capture it, but she wouldn't be able to tell if she'd succeeded unless she could take a closer look on her laptop.

The first time, he'd been looking across the harbor at a group of colorful sailboats drifting by, their sails billowing in the wind. A lazy afternoon on the water. There'd been something wistful in his gaze. She hoped she'd caught it, and also hoped she'd caught what she'd understood of him in that moment – the dreamer in him.

As they'd been getting ready to leave, there'd been an older couple walking on the street. They'd been holding hands. She'd instinctively taken pictures of the couple, although she had hundreds already. It was her dream future. She wanted to grow old together with someone special. She couldn't think of anything nicer than to sit on a veranda with her partner, together in rocking chairs, enjoying the passage of time, full of memories of their life together.

She'd caught sight of Kane's gaze on the same couple as they walked away. Sure, there was a bit of wistfulness there, but his gaze held more than a hint of regret for something just out of his reach. She'd been unable to resist taking several shots. A man like him had to have had a full and rich relationship history, but chances were also good that something had gone wrong with one of them. And that whatever had gone wrong was the major reason he was here.

There was a fury inside this man, but not against everyone. She definitely felt like it was directed at one particular person, most likely at his last relationship.

Or possibly…at himself.

As she sat there waiting for him to walk around and cool down from his last set of exercises, she wondered what could have gone so wrong as to send him to this place. It wasn't exactly AA therapy, but it was a specialized type of session for those who needed a different approach. As she hadn't been able to see the benefit for herself and had needed Jillian, her best friend, to point out how this could be her answer, she wondered who had shown Kane this next step in his journey.

Because he didn't look like he could see it for himself – especially not here and now.

She was due for a one-on-one session with Jenna this evening. She had to admit, she was looking forward to it. She had something to say, some new insight into her life, her mind, her way of looking at the world. And as much as she didn't want to dwell on Kane, some mention of her inscrutable partner was inevitable. She didn't want Jenna to know there was a definite physical attraction to Kane but thought the therapist would be able to figure it out within a few moments of Tania opening her mouth.

And that would be embarrassing.

She could feel her cheeks heating up at the thought of trying to explain herself. Now her friend Jillian would be screaming for joy, and she was tempted to text her friend and mention the hottie partner, but that would also start a long string of questions demanding answers.

And she didn't want to go there right now.

Or ever.

This was special, kinda like the first stirrings of long-dead hormones. Tania had tried to find other men attractive, but one couldn't force something like that. She didn't know why now. She couldn't submerge the constant need to look Kane's way and see what he was doing; the need to wonder about his story, his life, or any number of other issues going on. That awareness…that heat…that instinctive knowing where he was at any given time.

This was new for her, and she felt rubbed raw, super-sensitized to his presence. He must know. Maybe he could sense it. How humiliating. She felt like an overgrown teenager with awakening awareness of him.

She knew it had to be the circumstances. The setting. The project throwing them together in close proximity. It couldn't be real. She shook her head.

She smiled, feeling a release of tension across her shoulders.

This was just a moment in time. A passing thought.

"What's up?"

Startled, she looked over at Kane, now with a towel around his neck and wiping the sweat off his red face. He'd been working out while she'd been lost in thought.

She hopped to her feet. "I am so sorry. I was daydreaming."

"Yeah?" He tilted his head to study her. "About what?"

Willing the heat to stop its rapid climb up her neck, she stood up and fiddled with her camera. "Just life. The issues that brought me here. Things I want to take away from here."

He raised an eyebrow. "Glad you're getting something out of this."

"So are you." She grinned. "You're getting fit."

"Ha." He dropped the towel. "I am fit. There's no *getting* in this equation."

"Yeah, well, it seems to me you missed one rep on that last round."

He stared at her in mock outrage. "How would you know? You were sitting there like some kind of decoration, daydreaming. I'm the one working out here."

"And you'd better get back to it and make up your set," she said smoothly. She lifted her camera. "And this time, I'll be sure to catch every grunt and muscle movement."

He froze, a look of horror on his face. "You don't have audio on, do you?"

She laughed. "Nope. Just kidding. But I run a mean camera, which means I'll catch every little trick you try to avoid getting your full workout."

Good-naturedly, he returned to the huge set of weights and, starting with his right arm, he lifted a barbell she'd never be able to lift with two hands and started bicep curls.

She grabbed her camera and went to work herself.

When he stopped the next time, she noticed a change in his attitude. The look on his face. She bent closer, not quite understanding but wanting to – at least from behind the camera. It was as if he was exhausted but determined to continue. To force his body past this wall.

She didn't understand the will to do this. Why? Why would anyone, male or female, *want* so much physical pain and do yet more damage? She didn't understand how muscle building worked at this level. She understood it had something to do with creating tears in the fibers and having your body rebuild bigger, better, stronger.

But at this point...no, way earlier...she'd have walked

away.

Instead, he was heading into this next set as if this was now…finally…serious business! As if everything else was a warm-up to this.

She leaned closer.

His face twisted with concentration, and his gaze flattened – those don't-mess-with-me cop eyes she'd seen flickered in the dark-chocolate depths. And he reached deep inside and pulled those damn weights up again.

She could see his pain. Hear his pain. Feel his pain, yet still he pushed himself to reach for that goal.

In the end, she was so absorbed in the intensity of his own moment that she completely forgot to take pictures at the final point before he hit the wall…and went over it. She lost her balance and fell on her butt, camera in hand, mouth open as she stared at him.

He ever so slowly lowered the massive weight as if everything in him wanted to drop it and he wouldn't give in to it.

He was all about control.

And goals.

And making them.

Pushing himself, forcing himself to face his own weakness was everything to him.

And she knew in that moment, in ways she couldn't understand, that this man would never allow himself to hurt another person through a moment of weakness. It was not to say that in an equal fight in a boxing ring he wouldn't enjoy pulverizing his opponent, because she thought he would love that.

But he'd never take advantage. Never hit a woman, a child, or another man in anger.

She knew he'd never abuse someone or take advantage of

his superior strength.

But she wasn't sure *he* knew it. That when he lost it, when red took over his emotions and rage replaced the blood in his veins, he might shove his fist through a wall, but he'd never mistake a woman's face for that wall.

And he'd never, ever use force on a woman in other ways. He wouldn't have to. He would naturally see a lot of action, if he wanted it, but he wouldn't force a woman. He was a protector, not a predator.

With that thought, a band loosened around her chest, and the tension from just being this close to him eased back into the realm of normalcy. She'd been keeping a safe distance between them, being sure to avoid his touch, even accidentally. Something she'd done for years. Something she wasn't consciously aware of doing.

She sat quietly, contemplatively, while he collapsed and worked to regain his breathing.

How foolish she'd been. Walking the safe road may have been the way to go in the past, but she'd hit a turning point. She could trust her instincts that said he was safe to be around, or she could continue on this safe pathway and not give herself a chance to get a little closer to a strong, sexual male.

Her body said to jump his bones, but she was light years away from something so obvious. And so was he. He'd given no sign he was interested in her at all, and he had a lot more experience with sexual attraction than she had. He didn't seem to notice she was acting any differently.

So maybe she wasn't.

She lifted the camera and captured the sense of satisfaction, glowing exhaustion…pride.

Click. Click. *Click.*

WHAT COULD SHE possibly find to take pictures of after so many shots? She'd been going crazy with her damn camera. He'd blocked her out as he put himself through the pacing. He needed this workout, and all the more now because of her bouncing around. She'd gotten quiet once or twice. She'd called it daydreaming. He wasn't so sure, but it was weird.

Still, he needed to focus, needed this release of tension, of the uncomfortable situation. He wanted to be home in his space, in his gym…and work.

He had homework to do, cop work to do, getting his degree to do. He loved being a cop. He just wanted to do more. That's why he was here. Right? No, it was *one* of the reasons. His temper had been blowing louder and hotter. His personal issues had bled over into his work life, and that was when he'd understood he couldn't hold off doing something about this. He wanted a personal life, but he needed to work. And he couldn't afford to give his personal issues any more time to do their own thing on their own time – not once it had crossed into his work arena.

Then there was his brother.

Jessie had convinced him to take this step, to commit the time, energy, and intention to make this happen.

No one had warned him about the other people in the session – like Tania.

Then again, how did one prepare for such a thing?

He reached up and rubbed his face. The workout had done its job. He was exhausted. He was mentally and physically done; he was at the calm place where he was fine. Everything in his life was going to be okay. God, he loved this space.

It felt like home.

Centered. Balanced.

Peaceful.

Some people would say he was a gym junkie. That it was an addiction. If it was, he didn't want to get over it. There were truly few places he could go to and get this feeling, and even fewer ways to get there.

He needed this.

And now he felt like he could handle the world again.

Even Tinkerbelle.

"Surely you have enough pictures by now?"

She froze. "If you're done, then I do." She straightened and busied herself putting away her gear.

"Well, I need a shower," he joked. "So unless you're planning to document that…"

There was a tiny gasp. He spun around and realized she'd frozen in place, her eyes huge. But it was what churned in the back of those eyes that made him add, "Hey, I was just joking."

She blinked once again…and then she started babbling. "Sorry, I'm late. Need to go…back to my room. It's almost dinnertime." The whole time the words tumbled out of her mouth, she was backing up to the door, putting as much distance between them as she could.

At the door, she opened it and turned around as if to say something. Her face worked while he stood there with his mouth open, then she closed her lips and bolted.

The door slammed closed behind her.

CHAPTER 7

P ANIC DROVE TANIA to the stairwell. She sprinted up the first flight of stairs and turned the corner to the next. When she remembered she and Kane had rooms on the same floor and he could be coming behind her, she could hardly breathe.

She hated being a fool, and after that crazed exit, how could he see her as anything but?

Moving as fast as she could force her body, she raced up the stairs, desperately wanting to make the safety of her room before meeting him again.

Two flights up, she barreled into the middle of a group of older people as they bunched up at a landing.

"Sorry, excuse me." She apologized and tried to get through them.

They were laughing and trying to move but as one moved away to make space for her, another accidentally blocked her way. Finally, she stopped, blew her errant strand of hair out of her eyes, and waited until they'd all moved past her down the stairs. After a long moment, she resumed her upward climb at a slower, steady pace.

The jolt of meeting those people somehow made her see her actions for what they were: silly fears. So what if she did see Kane on the way?

If he thought she was panicked at the idea of her taking

pictures of him in a shower, then fine. What did it matter to her? Besides, it was better than the truth.

She opened the door on the third landing and walked calmly out to the hotel hallway. It was empty. She fished her key card out and unlocked her door.

With a last glance around, she entered her room and locked it behind her. She sagged against her door and closed her eyes.

"Christ," she whispered. From the moment Kane had suggested she take pictures of him in the shower, she had been beset by images of him standing nude with water sluicing down over his magnificent body. Water droplets hitting, hanging suspended for a moment like a lover's touch before sliding down over those curves and hard planes.

After today, she knew him so much more than he'd understood. She'd seen him both physically and mentally through the lens of a camera and although most people wouldn't understand, a camera never lied. It had the ability to capture moments of truth.

One of those truths couldn't be denied. He was a magnificent male in his prime. What he'd taken as fear in her eyes had actually been desire. A need to do just what he'd suggested. She'd give damn near everything she owned if she could, right at that moment, take a camera into his bathroom and photograph him in the shower.

And what did that say about her?

"It says you're a healthy female who met up with someone who sparked your attraction. It is new for you. It's also a good sign," she said out loud. *Bull.*

After a long, cooling shower, Tania curled up in a tight ball, her hair wrapped up in a towel, the housecoat miles too big on her small frame, cell phone clutched in her hand.

Feeling guilty, almost dirty, she'd completed her shower in record time and called Jillian.

"You don't understand. I ran from him. The words I wanted to say wouldn't come out. My heart was pounding." Tania stared around the cold hotel room and wanted to cry. "I'm sure he thought I was terrified of him."

"And instead, you were terrified of your reaction to him." Jillian gave a delighted laugh and said, "You are going through something most women go through in their teenage years and honestly, even now when I have a new relationship, I'm exactly the same."

"But I don't have a relationship with him," Tania said in exasperation. "I just made a fool of myself. The last thing he's going to want is a relationship with me."

"So? Women make fools of themselves over men all the time and vice versa. Understand it's normal. It's natural. In fact, it's a damn good sign. Be as natural as you can be. You're attracted to him. It's going to feel like high school for a while, but you will handle it." Jillian sounded so positive and happy that it gave Tania hope.

"I hope you're right. I feel like he'll never talk to me again."

Laughter filled the phone line again. Everyone loved Jillian – especially men. If she said this was normal even for her after all the relationships she'd had…then maybe it was.

"He'll talk to you. That's the great thing about where you are and what you are doing. He can't avoid you. He's part of the seminar, too." Then she sobered up slightly. "Just make sure he's not some damn wife beater or alcoholic, will you? You need a nice, stable, caring man to be in your life. Not someone with huge problems of his own."

"Everyone has problems here," Tania said. "I don't know

which of his brings him here."

"Well, he's in therapy, so look around at the hotel guests and staff. Maybe there's a different man, one without the huge baggage a man in therapy might have."

At that, Tania laughed. "Really? So a man who's willing to step up to deal with his issues is a worse bet than some guy in the bar who won't even look at them?"

"No. And if the therapy was over and this guy had done what he'd needed to do, he'd probably be a great bet. In the meantime, remember everyone is part of the session for a reason." Jillian's voice deepened with worry. "Especially him."

"What? You don't even know him," Tania said in outrage. "Don't be so judgmental."

"I'm not trying to be, but you…you're an innocent in life. And someone is likely to take advantage of you."

Shivers rippled down Tania's spine. As long as it was Kane, she just might be okay with that.

"It's too early. You don't know this man. You need more than a one-night stand."

"Do I?" she whispered. "What if you're wrong there? It would allow me to test drive sex as to whether I can do it or not. Then if it doesn't—"

"If it doesn't work, you're going to be even more traumatized." Jillian's voice turned pleading. "Please, don't do this. Flirt a little, enjoy the sensation of feeling that kind of heat, revel in knowing that your body is responding…but do not jump into bed with him – at least not yet."

Tania hung up on her. Her hand trembled as she stared in shock at the closed phone. She'd never hung up on anyone before. She collapsed to the bed and let the tears run. After a few moments, when the sobs died down, she stood up and went to the bathroom to wash her face. She took a drink of water and stared at her teary face in the mirror.

"God, I hate when I do something wrong." Especially to Jillian. It wasn't her fault Tania was screwed up, but it was because of her that Tania was here trying to work through everything.

Resolutely, she returned to the bedroom and dialed her friend back.

"I'm sorry," she said before Jillian could speak. "I had no right to do that."

"Of course you did," Jillian sighed heavily. "I'm sorry for pushing you to the point you felt it was the only answer."

"I didn't want to hear what you were trying to say."

"Yeah, I got the message." Jillian's voice lifted from sadness to humor, making Tania smile.

"I just feel so…" she shrugged. "I don't know. I feel alive; different, confused but almost hot."

Now Jillian broke into her beautiful, lilting laugh. "You sound so normal. I'm so happy you called me. I hadn't expected this type of progress, but there's no doubt that's what I'm seeing." She added a smirk in her voice. "I guess I hadn't expected it to show this way."

"I had no expectations," Tania laughed. "Who could?"

"Just…be careful," Jillian dropped her voice. "Please. You're very special, and you've been hurt enough."

"True. And I'm not going to do anything stupid. At least I'm not trying to. If I get a chance to take this one step further…well, I don't know, but I honestly don't think I could go through with it and to have me run from him at that stage could hurt him – badly, depending on his issues." In fact, it was likely to devastate him. And he'd come here to heal, too. She didn't need to screw his world up more just because she was a mess.

"That's the thing about sexual attraction; what looks great at night time when the heat is coursing through your veins can look horrible in the morning. Worse because, in the cold light of day, we look in the mirror and hate ourselves, realizing we'd done something we wouldn't normally do. In the morning, our actions are hard to live with. But that mirror is one we have to look at every day."

There was such a serious tone in her voice, and Tania realized she didn't know all of her friend's dark secrets, either. Obviously, Jillian had some experience with the less-than-nice side of sexual attraction.

She didn't know what to say. "I'm sorry. I don't know because I've never been there, but I hate to think you have such memories."

"Sweetie, most single women who've lived the singles life have a few of them. Some are easier to forget than others. In your case, I don't think you'd be able to forget. It would just compound other memories you can't walk away from, either."

"Damn. That's probably very true." Tania walked to the window and looked out. "In which case, I can just enjoy the benefit of knowing the seminar is working, and I'll come home a better, more complete person."

"Yes, you are, and you will. And that's awesome!" Jillian sighed happily. "I'm so happy to hear the seminar is working. Now I have to run. Go eat and enjoy the rest of the seminar. If anything else comes up, call me." She rang off.

In a better frame of mind, Tania glanced at her watch and understood she was going to be late for dinner if she didn't move it. She wasn't even dressed yet. Ten minutes later, dressed in slacks and a light, cashmere sweater with a little makeup on to hide the crying session, and she was ready to go. She grabbed her purse, her hotel card, and walked out, damn near walking into Kane.

"Whoa. Easy there." He reached out and grabbed her arms to steady her. "I know its dinner time, but you don't have to rush. They will save you some."

Her barely-leashed hormones took one look at that smorgasbord of delight in front of her, and a second appetite surged to life.

KANE HELD TANIA slightly apart from him and studied her features. She'd regained her balance physically, but something appeared to have set her off emotionally. He stared into her blue eyes, watching them darken. Why? She wasn't struggling to get away from him, but her pupils were dilated and her body swayed closer.

His own body woke up. He dropped his hands and stepped back slightly, and he smiled down at her. "Hey, you okay?"

She visibly tried to pull herself together. "Yeah, I'm fine. Sorry." She gave a headshake. "I have to watch where I'm going. I came out of my room and you surprised me."

"I'm just hoping to get dinner before it's too late."

On cue, her stomach growled. She gasped, and then laughed. "I guess my stomach has the same concern."

He grinned, happy to see her calming down and relaxing a bit. She was tense, had been most of the time he'd known her, except when she had the camera in her hand. Then she became someone else.

He motioned for her to precede him. She did, somewhat. She walked a half step in front of him, not quite comfortable that he was behind her. He walked, watching as she walked half-twisted as if to keep an eye on him.

Weird.

He took several larger steps to walk beside her, and she stopped trying to look behind her while she walked.

He wondered if she'd been attacked from behind at some point. He hadn't noticed this behavior before, but then he wasn't sure, and he cast his mind back to try and remember if he'd ever been behind her. He had, but he'd been a ways behind, like earlier this afternoon when she raced back to the hotel, not on her heels like this. And that appeared to be the problem.

He filed the tidbit away for later. He'd seen enough victims in his life to recognize some of the signs, but Tania was different. There were some things she couldn't hide, like when they'd first met. He was used to his size raising eyebrows. He'd also experienced some uncomfortable shuffling away when he sat down, like on an airplane, where people expected him to take up more than his single seat.

But in her case, she'd had the same reaction to him whether he'd been standing or sitting. As she was tiny, he figured she just felt dwarfed.

He'd seen it before. Some women liked a big man because it made them feel small and protected, while other women felt overpowered.

She reached over and pushed the elevator button, and then stepped back to give him space.

It was starting to piss him off.

When the elevator arrived, he stepped in first and slouched against the back wall, crossing his arms across his chest. He wouldn't want her to think he was going attack her in here.

The small elevator moved swiftly, but not fast enough for him to miss the worried glances she shot his way. He stared at the ceiling, feeling the same old burn inside build as old anger issues came to the forefront. His mood went downhill quickly as past grievances swamped him.

Damn females. Why couldn't they just be honest? Instead, they did this dance back and forth, always sending a guy from one side to the other. Being liars and cheats naturally, he figured the chances of finding a straight-arrow female to be impossible. It wasn't in their DNA. They were naturally wily and were born to manipulate. Most used their beauty to blind the poor male they were currently with.

Tania was a prime example, sending out all the right signals then immediately changing those signals so he had no clue what was going on. She was attracted to him, no way he could have missed those signals, but to look at her now…Christ.

The door opened at the restaurant lobby level. She walked out and headed to the restaurant, with another group stepping between them. They must have come from the stairwell. He was hungry, but at this point he wasn't sure he could eat. He stepped out of the elevator, walked to the front door, and stepped outside. The sun was still high, but with the buildings around, there were long shadows deepening the sky.

"Kane?"

He stiffened. Jenna. Of course, she'd be the one to find him. He was in a perfect mood to give her hell, too. He turned and stared at her, his jaw clenching at the narrow assessing gaze she locked on him.

"Hey." He tried for casual and curious.

And understood when her all seeing, all knowing gaze

narrowed even more that he'd failed. He sighed then straightened. "What's up?"

"How are you doing?" she asked calmly as she walked a few steps closer. "I don't see you looking for dinner yet. Not hungry?"

He was hungry, but food wouldn't satisfy this appetite. Damn Tania. With a sigh, knowing the therapist would see what she'd see, he said, "I was just getting a little fed up with Little Miss Rabbit always backing away, staring behind her as if afraid I was ready to attack at any moment."

Jenna's eyebrow shot up. "I hadn't realized she felt so intimidated. She's been doing so well."

That made him feel like shit, and he was a fair guy. "She is."

The therapist studied him for another moment, her expression lightening with understanding. "Ah. So maybe you're the problem."

He glared at her. "I'm fine."

She smiled. "I'm glad to hear that." She linked arms with him and tugged him back toward the restaurant. "I haven't eaten. Come and join me."

He didn't bother resisting. He was here to get help and as she'd said, he was the problem.

And that just sucked.

Before he knew it, he was seated at a table and ordering dinner. And damn if Tania wasn't seated next to him.

Had Jenna arranged that on purpose? He shot her a questioning look.

She smiled, reached over, and patted his arm. "Enjoy. The food here is a delight."

Tania, from the other side, leaned forward and said, "It is indeed. I'm really enjoying the visit here. It's a lovely location for healing."

Jenna leaned in closer to talk to Tania as if he wasn't there. He leaned back so they could see each other while they spoke across him.

Then when the faintest whiff of Tania's perfume drifted across his face, that was when he recognized he really didn't want to be anywhere else.

CHAPTER 8

W HAT WAS KANE'S problem? Tania had hoped he had not noticed her flustered state as they came down. He'd seemed normal enough, yet when she'd come walking into the restaurant worrying about where she should sit – beside him or a long ways away – she found out he hadn't followed her in.

Talk about a letdown. She'd been staring at the damn entranceway watching for him since.

When he'd sat down beside her, she'd been delighted until she realized he'd sat at the last empty chair and then had seemed surprised to see her beside him.

So much for the hope that he might be attracted to her. He didn't even know she existed.

Determined to be friendly regardless, she pasted a smile on her face and kept it there. Robin was on the other side. Halfway through dinner, Robin caught her eye and motioned toward the washroom. Taking her cue, Tania excused herself and followed Robin to the ladies' room.

As soon as the door closed behind them, Robin exploded. "What is going on with you?"

Tania stared at her in shock. "Huh?"

"Your face has been a movie all through dinner. You sat down and looked happy, then looked around and your face fell. Jenna and Kane walk in and you light up. Then something odd happened and you looked like you'd taken a major hit. Now, it's as if you're trying to hide something or trying to avoid something...hell...I don't know...but it's like you're trying too hard to not be affected by whatever is bothering you."

With the outburst over, she leaned against the counter and dropped her head back. "Normally, I wouldn't say anything, but whatever is going on has to do with Kane, and damn it, girl, you are a guppy in a sea of sharks. And Kane could turn out to be the king of the Great White Sharks."

In a small voice, Tania said, "I was that obvious?"

"Yes, you were," Robin said in a short voice. "I know we're all here dealing with shit. And it's private shit. Hell, I don't want all my dirty laundry hanging out for everyone to see, but you're glowing like a kid right now."

Tania walked over so she could stare into the mirror. There was no glow now, only bruises. This day had been tough, and it looked like it wasn't over. She didn't know what to say; surely the red all over her face said enough. Robin turned to stare at her in the mirror.

She sighed, and in a much gentler voice, she said, "I'm sorry. I didn't mean to hurt you. But your erratic behavior is like a neon sign. It never does any good to let a man know you are too interested. Interested, yes, but that you have no resistance to the attraction – no."

"It's all so difficult. I've never felt anything like this. Hadn't ever expected to, and now... now, I have no idea how to handle it." She ran her fingers through her hair, wanting to grab on and pull it out. "Apparently I'm not doing a good job of it."

"Just relax. Be yourself. Don't try to impress him. Don't worry if he doesn't like something you say or do. All relationships are improved when the two people involved are honest, both with themselves and each other."

Robin studied her own features in the mirror. "Before this," she motioned to the ruined side of her face, "I had several really good relationships. Keeping a relationship going is an art…maybe that's where I fall down. But you have to get one to learn how to keep it. And you're sending off signals that would confuse the hell out of any guy."

Tania's mouth fell open. "Wait. You just said I was too eager."

"And too confused. He wasn't there the whole time, so he didn't see the gambit of emotions flashing across your face for the last hour. Just calm down. If it's meant to be, it's meant to be." She shrugged.

"And the shark and guppy comment?" Tania said drily. Inside, she just felt tired, like her first foray had been bad enough that she should go to her room and forget all about Kane.

"He's a big, sexy male, and he knows it. You are a tiny, sexy female, and you don't know it."

Tania smiled. "I can see that."

"Sharks have their purposes in the ecosystem, too. Maybe he's learning to be a relationship man… Look, all I'm saying is I wouldn't want you to jump into anything and get hurt." She walked to the door. "Now, let's go finish our meal."

With the second person in as many hours warning her to tread carefully, Tania realized they just might know what they were talking about. Subdued, she returned to her chair and finished her plate.

"Tania, are you ready for a session tonight?"

Unfortunately, Jenna's question appeared to fall into a

moment of silence at the table.

Tania froze. She worked to keep her face calm, but inside, her mind screamed *hell no!* The last thing she wanted was a third woman warning her to back off. She'd gotten the message. She chewed slowly while she considered her answer. The therapist would analyze everything she said, a failing of the profession.

"I'm really tired tonight. How about in the morning?" she said quietly.

She felt the heat of Jenna's gaze as she cut up a piece of chicken and ate it. When she raised her gaze to look at the therapist, Jenna smiled. "Sure, sounds good. How about a breakfast meeting? 7-ish?"

"That's early, but sure…at least I'll be awake for tomorrow's class."

Jenna smiled. "Good. Until the morning then." With a smile at everyone, Jenna stood up and took her leave.

Almost instantly, a tension Tania hadn't been aware of before eased. The teacher left the room and the kids were now relaxing. She grinned.

"Hey, what are you smiling at?" Robin asked with a big smile. "You appear to be in a good mood."

"Yeah, I pushed that meeting off until the morning." Tania grinned. Maybe she shouldn't have, but she needed rest from the emotional overload, and a part of her wanted to see if Kane had plans for the evening and if they included her. As that was the wrong thing to be waiting for, she decided to go up to her room. Standing up, she excused herself. "I have homework to do."

Kane looked up at her. "Are you going to go through the pictures?"

She nodded. "Yes, to see if I can find any worth keeping."

"Do you need help?" he asked, half-straightening from his chair.

"No." At the surprised look on his face, she gave a small laugh. "At least not at this stage. There are hundreds of shots, and I'm most likely to delete ninety percent of them. When the numbers get down to something reasonable, then I'll show you and you can go through the ones I think might work."

He grinned. "In other words, you don't want me to see the less-than-stellar pictures."

"So true." She waved goodbye to the others and headed up to her room. Once inside, she brought out her laptop and started downloading the pictures. She had no idea how many she'd taken; only that she'd gone madly click-happy. The file was huge. She walked to the side counter and made herself a cup of coffee. She could have stayed longer, but she was happy to have time alone, time to find her balance again. Having one's behavior pointed out took a bit of adjustment. At twenty-four, she wasn't a kid any longer, but apparently she still didn't know how to behave in public. She could put the blame for that squarely on Kane's shoulders.

Kane's beautiful shoulders.

If she had to do a photography class and would not be able to choose her own subject, Kane made a hell of a second choice.

Hell, who was she kidding, Kane *was* her first choice.

Finally, the file was downloaded. She sat down with her coffee, opened her image program, and quickly started sorting through the pictures. She did a quick go-through and deleted the ones that were obviously junk, then went back through the remaining hundred. She created a file titled

"Project" and dropped several good images into that folder. There was one of Kane standing and staring at the sailboat. She loved the way the camera had caught the wistfulness in his eyes. She plowed through the next group and picked out a couple that caught his hard jaw as he stared at something off screen. She chose the images that spoke to her. They said something about Kane, the man. The camera loved him, making it that much harder to sort through the last thirty images in the file. When she was done, she turned her attention to the group of pictures she'd taken while he'd worked out.

That was when she understood how the camera not only loved Kane, but that his body was made for this. All the beautifully defined muscles, the ripples as they moved and shifted…she wished for the first time that she had a video camera. He was a man in motion. Such a connection. In one shot, his jaw clenched, and his eyes were so focused. There was one of his bicep, the muscle so smooth and shiny but hard and tense with the effort he was exerting.

She put one of her favorite photos into a different folder she named "Special". Kane had just finished the workout; he'd collapsed back down to the mat. In her mind, she remembered the heaving chest, the quivering look at the hard muscle, but it was the look of relief, the look of pride, and that tinge of complacency as he realized he'd done it. He'd managed to complete his physically punishing workout again. He hadn't let it beat him.

She knew it was a competition for him. A challenge to see if he was up to it or if he was going to wuss out. He would not appreciate her thoughts, she was sure, but he had such a sense of satisfaction around him that she could only cheer with him. As she went through the pictures from start to finish, it was as if she was there all over again. Seeing the pain, the effort he exerted, hearing the grunts and gasps as he struggled to make his body do what he wanted it to do.

His skin glowed in one particular picture. She considered it, wondering at the light that hit and bounced off his skin. A sheen of sweat had appeared just before she'd taken the shot and as she studied the next couple of pictures, she understood that the reflection had added something else to the picture. Like a mirror of what he was doing to himself.

She loved this one. Setting it aside, she moved through several more, but they were more mundane, showing his actions but not the highs and lows, not the emotion or the effort. They were technically good, but flat. She set them into another folder she named "Kane".

She wouldn't be keeping them but as they were good shots, just not great shots, she'd let him see them and decide for himself.

There were still a few more. Another one had an interesting light as it hit Kane's back and the muscles gleaming in the shadows. Very inspiring.

She snorted. Who was she kidding? The man was damn sexy and maybe there was something wrong with her, but the sweaty, hardworking man apparently did it for her.

Who knew?

And wasn't that something? She savored the warmth. Screw that, savored the *heat* coursing through her body as she stared at the pictures of Kane. Salivating was a bit much, but she had to admit, she wanted a taste of him.

She'd never thought to have gotten this far. Now that she had, everyone was warning her away.

Would having an affair with Kane be wrong? No.

And as she stared down at him, reality once again

crashed down on her. She could sit here and dream all she wanted; it was still a hell of a long ways from actually lying down with the man.

She buried her face in her hands. She was a mess.

Of course she was. She was here in a goddamned therapy session, wasn't she?

Wiping back the tears from the corner of her eyes, she finished sorting through the pictures. As she came back to the one that had set her off earlier, she copied it into a folder she named "Secret". She almost felt dirty doing it, but if there was only one thing she could take away from this week, it was these pictures of Kane. Although he hadn't said she could keep them after the project was done.

Sighing, she went to turn off her laptop when there was a casual knock on her door.

She stood up and walked to the door. "Who is it?" she asked. She hated peepholes and never used them to look outside. She'd seen too many movies showing horrors on the other side of the damn door.

"Kane."

Oh shit.

She straightened her shirt, brushed her hair back off her face, and opened the door. "Hey."

He smiled down at her. "Just came to see if you got through those photos. We're both in the project, remember? You don't have to do all the work."

She laughed. "No, I won't. I'm still not sure what this damn project is supposed to be or how it's going to help."

He started to step inside before he stopped and looked at her. "May I come in?"

TANIA TOOK A deep breath and stepped aside. She followed him into her room. Here was another first. She'd never had a man in her bedroom, and she'd never had a man this close in a very long time.

"I'd like to see the pictures you took."

She nodded and disconnected her laptop. "Fine. Do you want to go to the coffee shop and look at them?"

He tilted his head and motioned to the small table where the laptop rested. "I thought I could just look at them here. It won't take long, will it?"

Disconcerted, she plugged in her laptop in. She shook her head. "No, it shouldn't. I deleted the bulk of them." She bent down, found the folder, and opened it.

He pulled the desk chair back far enough to be able to sit down. He leaned forward slightly and clicked through the images in her program. He studied each one carefully, stopping longer at one or two then moving past several as if they weren't as visually impressive. She knew they weren't all good, but she had to have something to start with.

He came to the end and studied the last one, the picture where he'd completed his workout, the pain, the suffering, but also the gain he'd achieved on so many levels.

"You're very intuitive."

She started. That's the last thing she'd expected. "Pardon?"

He waved at the pictures. "In fact, I'd have to say you're very gifted."

He'd surprised her, too. "I'm good, but not *that* good."

He snorted. "You see more behind a lens than you give yourself credit for." He clicked back a couple of pictures. "While you were taking pictures, I couldn't think of what you'd possibly find interesting when I was repeating the same movements over and over again. But you weren't taking pictures of the movements, but of *me* as I went through them."

She stared at him. "So? What else was I to take pictures of?"

He grinned. "That's what I was trying to figure out. You captured more of me in these images than I thought was there to see."

He stood up. "On top of it all, the play of light and dark is interesting."

"We're supposed to do a theme of some kind, a journey." She studied the thumbnail pictures lined up in neat rows on the folder and twisted her lips. "There's not much there to go on."

"No," he said in a deep voice. "But I suspect there's enough."

He walked to the door.

She trailed behind him. "Does that mean you understand the instructions Jenna gave us? About a theme?"

"It means that I think I'm beginning to." He looked down at her. "Get some sleep, Tinkerbelle. You're going to need it."

Then he was gone.

CHAPTER 9

THE NEXT MORNING dawned bright and early. Tania woke up with Kane on her mind, which was to be expected, although the dreams had bordered on erotic but in a fantasy way. Not realistic, and that was also to be expected. The man wasn't for her, and a relationship wasn't likely to happen, therefore her subconscious had kept it in fantasy. But she could still dream.

Throwing back the covers, she remembered her early morning meeting with Jenna, and damn if she wasn't going to be late. She threw on clothes and ran.

At the coffee shop, Jenna sat with a pot of tea at her side, an open notebook in front of her and a look of concentration on her face.

Tania almost hated to interrupt.

As if sensing her presence, Jenna lifted her head and caught sight of Tania. A smile broke across her face.

Tania admitted that a smile from her stunning professor was like being brushed by a ray of sunshine. Tania didn't know Jenna's story, but somehow she'd arrived at a beautiful place in her life, and it showed.

Tania took a seat at Jenna's table. "Sorry I'm late."

Jenna shrugged. "If being late meant you had a good night's sleep, then there's no loss. It's not as if I've been waiting long."

The waiter arrived then, giving Tania a chance to order coffee and something to eat. She had an appetite, she realized with surprise. She'd expected to be so overwrought this morning that food wouldn't sit well, but instead she felt fine. Great, in fact.

"You look well this morning," Jenna said, a look of pleased surprise on her face. "Obviously, this week isn't stressing you out too badly."

Tania gave her a quirky smile. "Actually, it is, but in ways I hadn't expected. I also hadn't expected to feel so upbeat this morning, but there you have it."

With that, the two women started a discussion of yesterday's homework. When done, Tania understood a discussion of Kane and the project would likely be next. That sent a tremor through her. She had so much to say, yet she wasn't ready to say anything.

"How did yesterday afternoon go?"

"It was good." Tania grinned. "I enjoyed having a camera in my hand again. Kane is a great subject," she said, warming to the topic. "Some of the pictures are really unique."

"Excellent." Jenna smiled as she poured herself a cup of tea. "What have you learned so far?"

"He's easy to photograph; the camera loves him." She went into a discussion about trying to capture the different looks she'd seen in his eyes, the control he had and the drive to keep working out even when his muscles trembled with the effort.

"He's quite a man," she added soberly. "I don't know why he's here, but he's been very easy to work with." She added thoughtfully, staring out the window, "Maybe too easy."

"What makes you say that?"

"I think he sees me as damaged and himself as whole."

Jenna paused in the act of lifting her teacup to her mouth. "Interesting."

"He is. It's like he's only here on sufferance, but he's willing to do this if it will help me. But it won't help him because he doesn't have stuff. No..." Tania stopped. "More as if he has stuff to deal with, but this workshop isn't likely to help him deal with it, so he'll help me out in order to get through the week."

Jenna's eyes twinkled. "Another interesting observation."

Tania grinned. "All I'm doing is observing Kane."

Jenna stayed suspiciously quiet on that comment. Breakfast was served then, and the topic went to more general topics. Before she'd realized it, Tania was once again seated at the round table in the seminar room, waiting for the other attendees to show up.

And then Kane walked in.

Her spine rippled with awareness. She knew Kane had just walked in, and yet she hadn't even seen the man yet. She couldn't help the big smile on her face. She was both happy and excited, loving the feelings that lit her nerve endings along with the awareness of what was. This was all good, just as Jillian had said. It was good to feel this way; it felt right. As if she was finally normal in some way.

"Mind if I sit here?" Kane said, standing beside her. She smiled up at him, "No problem. There might be room." In fact, the chairs were bunched on the other side of her, leaving an abnormally large space for him.

He winked at her then sat down. Her gaze widened. She straightened up, thankful Jenna appeared just then to start their day off.

By noon, Tania was tired and cranky. There was nothing like listening to others talk about progress in their lives to make her feel like she'd made none. Regardless of how much progress she'd managed to create, it didn't look like it was enough. They broke for lunch and would resume working on their projects right after. Instead of eating, Tania headed outside for some fresh air. One of the men had several positive, uplifting stories to tell. She'd cheered with him and had fallen silent with the remaining members of the class when Jenna had asked if anyone else had something they wanted to share.

Yes, she wanted to share her news. She wanted to scream it out loud to anyone who'd listen. Her body was reacting like a normally functioning woman. She'd been in lust for her first time, felt that keen edge of a sword blade of attraction across her soul. It was good stuff – great stuff.

But it wasn't exactly shareable news.

"Not hungry?"

Tania turned. Kane had followed her out. "I just wanted some fresh air."

"In that case, why don't you grab your camera and we'll carry on where we left off and grab a bite to eat later?"

She opened her shoulder bag to show him the contents. "Already got it."

"Perfect." He walked down the pathway, and Tania raced to catch up. "Where do you want to go?"

"Out," came the laconic reply.

"Yeah, well, you've accomplished that today."

"I have. What's the next goal then? Yesterday, we followed my day. Today, we'll follow your day."

"Ha, in that case, we'd be studying all day."

He winced. "Then we'll need to find a midpoint between us."

"It's beautiful outside. We could just walk."

"There's a nice little Chinese restaurant down the boulevard a bit. How about we walk to our lunch?"

Feeling like they were sneaking away on a private lunch, Tania quickly agreed. She stopped just short of calling it a date in her head even though she really wanted to.

"Of course, you'll need to keep clicking that damn camera."

"I can walk, talk, and take pictures."

"Wow, a modern woman." His voice was teasing.

With light-hearted banter setting the tone, she took several pictures as he walked, having him stop and stand a few times so she could capture him with specific backgrounds. By the time they'd reached the restaurant, they were both arguing comfortably and Tania realized something else. It was the first time she'd spent any time alone in a man's company, and they'd been talking like old friends.

It was comfortable. Nice.

She didn't want it to end.

"LUNCH WAS GOOD, but I think I ate too much." Tania bounced at his side. Given their size difference, she had to almost run to keep up. "You barely ate," he scoffed.

"Ha, just because I'm not the size of a small mountain doesn't mean I didn't eat a lot."

He rolled his eyes. "Like I haven't heard that before."

"Sorry, I'm not used to this type of kibitzing." Her lips twisted wryly. "I need more practice."

That's when it hit him. She wasn't used to anything male-related. Talking like this, taking pictures, having a meal with a man. He half-suspected she'd never been on a date in her life. What he'd taken for fear had likely been just nervousness of being alone around males in general. She'd relaxed now, comfortable in his company.

Good.

"So, now what?"

"I don't know. We're about twenty minutes from the hotel, but you haven't taken many pictures yet. This means we have more homework to do."

She grew quiet at his side as they walked.

"What are you thinking?"

"I got a lot of pictures when you were working out, but I didn't get a couple that I'd been trying for."

"So you want me to go work out again?" Fine with him. Being around her was sending his libido off the wall. A workout would chase some of it back down to normal levels. Exhaust him so he could sleep at night. For all that he'd slept, his dreams had been heavy with Tinkerbelle content, and not in an innocent way. There had been nothing childish about those dreams.

"I don't know how often you work out. Maybe you don't do it every day, in which case, I'll wait until tomorrow."

"Except we're not going to have many days left."

She winced. "In that case…"

"Right, then back to my room to get my gear on."

"I'll meet you in the fitness room."

He slid her a sideways glance and realized she was trying to avoid being in his room. Too bad. That was starting to be the number one place he wanted her to be.

CHAPTER 10

T HE FITNESS ROOM was empty when Tania arrived. She'd been hoping it would be, not sure how she'd handle being watched as she photographed Kane working out.

She hadn't lied to him when she'd told him she'd missed a few images she'd hoped to have captured. Several of the images she'd kept were close but weren't good enough in her estimate. He gave so much of himself to his goals that she could do no less in her attempt to capture the same intensity of his expression.

She sat down and systematically went through the contents of her bag, mentally shifting through the options to take the best images. Being inside limited the experience – she'd love to have him swimming in a lake. See the water droplets run off his skin in the moonlight. This set of stills appeared to be all about light and dark. She paused, lifted her head, and considered the homework assignment. That could be the theme. It was certainly the essence showing through the images. When Kane walked into the room ten minutes later, she asked him.

"Light and dark?" he frowned as if considering it.

"Think of the images I showed you last night. And the way light plays on your skin, your muscles as they move. The reflections," she said encouragingly. "Can't you see it?"

"Fitness is more like it. I can see that as a theme."

She paused and slowly repacked her bag as she thought about it. He'd been joking, she'd been sure, but maybe it wasn't such a bad idea.

"I'm doing mostly legs today," he warned.

She stared at him then shrugged. "As that means nothing to me, I'll learn as you work."

And boy, did she learn.

He did a warm-up that had her aching with sympathy, and then he started doing lunges, squats, and a mess of other exercises she couldn't begin to understand. In an attempt to anticipate his muscles moving and bunching at the right time to catch with her camera, she bent, crouched, kneeled, and twisted in positions she couldn't normally get into to catch the right shots.

By the time he shifted to using a huge long bar with weights on either end, he'd settled into a comfortable rhythm and her body was starting to ache.

"How can you do this all the time?"

"I like it. I like to feel my body working at peak performance. It's a fine-tuned machine and like any machine, it needs to be worked out."

"I'm sore just from taking pictures," she muttered.

"Good. Helps you to remember you have muscles."

"Ha. I do yoga all the time."

"Good for you. I don't bend and twist well."

"Like this?" She put her camera down, stood in front of him, then bent forward from the waist while wrapping her right arm behind her to curl around her waist on the opposite side.

"See, now that's not normal." He shook his head but bent forward and tried to imitate her. His huge biceps didn't allow his arm to move well behind his back, and his palm could only go to his spine.

She grinned. "See those of us that can, do."

"Smart ass." Good-naturedly, he squatted to lift his bar.

She marveled at the cords running up and down his neck as he added more and more weights.

"How is this a leg workout?"

"It's now an all-over exercise, but the legs get a hell of a workout," he said when he could. "You've been taking pictures, which muscles are showing up the most?"

She waited until he lifted again and took a serious look. His quads looked like rippled granite, his arms almost the same. Without a shirt on as he'd taken that off some time ago, his six-pack popped out like crazy.

"It's so hard to say. All of you." She walked around behind him, loving the way his neck muscles worked and the shine that highlighted the hills and valleys of his body.

"Do you do these exercises all the time?"

"No. I have to work with what's here. Normally, I have someone who spots for me. So I'm doing only basic lifts here."

She nodded, preferring he didn't do anything that was dangerous. She might be able to lift the empty bar, but with all those discs on the end…she wouldn't be able to even roll it off him.

With his next set of lifts, the sweat started to pour. She watched as one bead rippled down his neck. Then another rolled off his spine.

Her camera went crazy.

And she knew she had to do something else.

She reached out and touched one on the side of his face.

A SECOND TINY drop of sweat rolled off his forehead to bounce onto his shoulder. Tania stood transfixed. Why?

"What's wrong?" Kane asked. He grabbed his towel and wiped the rest of the sweat off his forehead. He'd been working up a hell of a sweat this time. It seemed worse today. After last night. After seeing the pictures, he couldn't really explain it. It had been such an intimate look into him – his life, his body. It didn't bother him like a pervert watching him might have done. Knowing Tania was getting turned on was a hell of a turn on for him, too.

"Nothing," she said, her voice husky.

He snorted. "Well, something obviously is. Spill."

Mutely, she shook her head. "No. I'm fine. Sorry."

With a disgusted sound, he grabbed the bar again. He needed to do an extra rep, and that pissed him off. But better another rep than forcing the issue between them. There were too many damn issues between them.

And none of them solvable.

He'd been working up a sweat for a bit now. It felt good setting his rhythm, working his body, pushing it to do what it was meant to do.

Then she did something that caught the breath in the back of his throat.

She reached out and scooped up a drop of sweat onto her finger.

His groin tightened.

And damn if she didn't lick her finger.

He slowly lifted his gaze from her finger to her eyes. Their gazes caught and held.

Talk about a come on. But in her eyes, there was only curiosity and shock, and as he stared, he could see...desire.

CHAPTER 11

TANIA COULDN'T BELIEVE she'd just done that. And in front of him, no less. She might have gotten away with it if his back was turned to her or he was so busy as to not have noticed, but not this way. She swallowed hard.

God, she wanted him. There was no way to hide it now. He knew. He had to know. How could he not?

Fatalistically, she waited for him to speak.

"My room or yours?" he said, his voice deep, thick.

She closed her eyes and swallowed hard.

"Can't handle a direct approach?" he mocked, anger biting his tone.

Tears clogged her throat. Damn it. "You're probably right," she said in shame. She closed her eyes and shook her head. After a long, shaky breath, she said, "Sorry," her voice faint, barely above a whisper. "I can't."

She spun and ran to the exit. Outside the gym room, she ran up the stairs to the relative safety of her own hotel room. But there was no escaping the heat in her loins or the sweaty palms, and even worse, the images in her mind. She wanted what she couldn't have, needed what her body could never get, and it was making her crazy.

Shame coursed through her. Not for feeling desire, not for wanting a man, but for giving him the impression that he could have what he had good reason to expect at this point.

She hadn't been leading him on, but it might seem like it to him. He was a sexually active, healthy male. She was a damaged, broken female.

The two did not fit together. Regardless of the images in her mind telling her she was a liar, she knew it was true. He needed something healthy and whole. She needed…to let go of a dream.

Then someone knocked on her door.

KANE SLAMMED HIS fist into the wall.

Goddamn it. He felt like he'd just pulled off Tinker-belle's wings.

And he hadn't meant to. She got to him. He wanted to be man enough for her to play with and not give a damn, but he wasn't sure he could.

He wanted her like he hadn't wanted a woman in a very long time.

And she might want him, and she might think she was ready for this, but she wasn't, as he'd just proven.

Goddamn it.

Kane didn't know what he was going to say to her. He'd barely had a chance to figure out what the hell was going on here. She wanted him and he wanted her. Didn't that make for an easy solution? Apparently not. Women always complicated the simplest things.

The door opened in front of him, which surprised him. He'd figured she'd ignore him. Make their next meeting uncomfortable, where she'd retreat into herself and keep their relationship on a more formal level. Instead, she gave him a small smile, but the look of dread in her eyes made him realize she'd been churning up inside about this.

"Can I come in?"

Her mouth opened, but no words came out. Sighing, he pushed the door open slightly and stepped inside, almost forcing her to back up or be touched. Because that was really the problem here, wasn't it? He'd been slow to get it. Everything they'd done had been without physical contact. She'd gone out of her way not to touch him while they were seated or standing; she walked around him to get to the same place in an effort to not accidentally touch him. He'd only recognized it down in the fitness room, because after days of doing this, he finally understood that she'd only touched him – or anyone – once.

When she'd reached for that drop of sweat.

And it had hit him. He figured he understood the problem. He hoped she'd tell him the truth, but he didn't want to make her more uncomfortable. She had a look of doom on her face now as she led the way back into a close copy of his own hotel room. He avoided staring at the large bed in front of them. His body was too wired. It would be happy to head straight into sexual playtime, and as he'd had a hell of a time reining that back, seeing the wide expanse of a bed like this wasn't helping.

She turned to face him.

"What did you want to say to me?"

Her tone was polite and cold as if she was waiting for a blow, her shoulders hunched and her hands stuffed into her jeans pocket. As if she could get through this. She could get through anything if she had to.

He sighed, his determination to get to the bottom of this draining down to his toes. Who could stay mad at Tinkerbelle? Someone had to be an asshole to want to kick the woman when she was already down. He just didn't want her down for the wrong reason. Knowing he was likely to say the wrong thing but feeling the need to say something, he started with, "Look, I get that there is some trauma in your past. It's probably why you're here, since we're all here for something." He stopped. Her face had gone blank. Talk about giving an answer without saying anything.

He wanted to reach out and hold her. Give her a hug. Enclose her in his arms and tell her it would all be okay.

But she'd already learned that a touch wasn't always nice. That hugs were often a constraint and that life wasn't going to be okay. It would never be okay again.

"I get that you've been hurt, likely physically and emotionally, but I've never hurt anyone…especially a woman." Her gaze flew up to his, shock the dominant expression.

He started again. "You don't have to tell me what's going on, but the mixed signals were getting very confusing. But I want you to know that I got it. I'm slow and obviously thick, but I do understand. I'm not here to push you into doing something you don't want to do or aren't comfortable doing…"

She shook her head. "Maybe you aren't, but…"

She stopped.

He waited.

She dropped her head and stared at the floor.

"Okay, well. Look, I'm a big boy. I can handle a little sexual tension, a session of raw sexuality that isn't going where I'd like it to go." Her eyes flipped up to stare at him, then dropped to the floor again.

"I'm not going to jump your bones because you gave me a come-on. I'm not a callow youth who doesn't know his own limits, and I'd never do something you don't want me to do." When she continued to stare at the floor, he turned and walked back to the door before he stopped and turned back to face her. "I just wanted to let you know that I don't hold anything against you. If you feel brave enough to take the next step in this…" he waved a hand. "Whatever this is…I might be interested."

At her continued silence, he added, "Only, you're going to have to make it clear, because I can't take your actions like I would another woman's. So if you are, then just be honest and say so."

And he turned back to the door.

When he heard the single word, he stopped, puzzled. He turned back to face her. "What did you say?"

She took a deep breath and raised her eyes from the carpet to stare directly at him. In a tone of voice that said taking her medicine was good for her even if she didn't want it, she only wanted the benefits of it, she repeated what she'd said. "So."

His mind worked, trying to interpret her answer. Again, women seemed to make everything too complicated. "So, what?" he asked cautiously.

"I'm saying so."

And then he got it. His eyes closed. "Meaning you are interested in taking this another step and are saying so?"

"Yes."

So maybe this was simple after all.

"How far do you want to go?" He didn't know what he was up against, but this was unlike any conversation he'd ever had with a woman. There was no romance, no soft words, and no seduction. There was heat and raw, dry passion that crackled between them, something he hadn't ever felt. Not like this. It almost hurt, and the need was so strong it clawed at him. If it was the same for her, they'd burn up the sheets if they ever got there.

And again, she surprised him with her honesty. "I want it all," she said, "but I don't know what I can take."

"Take?"

"I was raped a long time ago," she said candidly, staring up at him. "I haven't been held by a man since. I couldn't. Not even my father." She bowed her head. He could just imagine the pain for both her and her father. It was a big admission.

A man? Interesting turn. The rape only confirmed what he'd already suspected. He was damn sorry for it, but he couldn't do anything about it at this point. "What about a brother?" She shook her head. "A good friend?"

"No. I have no males in my life, just two sisters and mother. My father and I talk on the phone, but he doesn't live close now."

He had to wonder at a life completely devoid of touch from the opposite sex. He had close relationships with his sister, brother, and both his parents. They hugged, touched, held hands; there were few physical boundaries between them because their relationships were founded on trust and respect.

She hadn't had the benefit of any male in her life since she was raped. Somehow, that made it all so much worse. "I'm sorry."

She shrugged. "It's been a long time." Her gaze slid to the side. "You think it's all good and you've dealt with it, but then something triggers the emotions and you realize it's not something you ever get over, or ever forget. It's not a sickness you can get rid of, but it is something you can deal with on a day-to-day basis. Like managing an incurable disease, it hurts at the oddest moments."

"Like?"

She smiled sadly, "Like when I see a family with babies or loving couples and I understand it's not for me. It's for people who have normal, natural lives. Not for those of us who are broken."

"You're in pieces, but you can pull the pieces together."

"But I'll never be whole."

"You can be better than you were," he said seriously. "You can be the new you."

Chapter 12

S HE COULDN'T BELIEVE they were having this conversation or that she'd had the guts to open up. Everyone – her friends, therapists, and family – had all said it would happen at one time, but why with Kane?

Except that if there was a chance in the immediate future for her to be intimate with a man, it would be with Kane. At least he now understood. She wasn't sure she did. What could he possibly want from her?

Except clearer signals, apparently.

He ran his fingers through his hair and stared at her, perplexed. She wanted to run her fingers through his hair, too, but he'd likely freak out.

"What?" He narrowed his gaze at her.

She dropped hers to the floor.

"Speak up. You have to be clear. I can't be helpful if you don't explain."

She laughed. "Ha. If you understood what I was thinking, you'd be running like a crazy man."

He tilted his head to one side. "Maybe not. Try me."

"No, it's stupid." She spun on her heels and walked so she could look out the window.

"Nothing is ever stupid. If you don't speak up, you will have missed an opportunity."

She glanced over at him. "It's just that I don't know

what your hair feels like." She turned away from him again. "See, I told you. It's stupid."

"You never touch me. You walk around me like I'm someone to avoid, as if my touch is repellent."

"No." She spun away from the window. "Not because of that, because…I don't know…I haven't touched a man, like I said. It's foreign and it's instinctive to *avoid* touching."

"But you want to touch?"

Tears filled her eyes, burning the back of her throat. They'd come on so hard and so fast, she hadn't been prepared.

"Oh no. No tears. That's not fair," he protested.

She tried to smile, but the waterworks kept getting in the way. "Sorry, I didn't mean to."

"Okay, so try this: just nod. Do you want to touch me?" He stood so big and so strong and so very capable of knocking her unconscious with a single blow, yet all she could think about was how much she wanted to touch him.

She nodded.

"See," he said in a very gentle voice. "That wasn't so hard."

"Was too," she muttered, but she smiled at him.

He walked over to a chair, flipped it around, and sat on it backwards, facing her. Sitting down, he was almost the same height she was. Then he dropped his head onto his arms resting on the back of the chair and said, "Go ahead."

"Why are you doing this?' she whispered. It was stupid. It was just a touch. But for her, it was a gift. A freedom she'd never had. And for him, this was what? An experiment? Wanting to help? Why was he here anyway? She hadn't seen or heard him do anything that explained why he'd needed to come to a workshop like this. Or was he not an attendee?

Had he come at Jenna's request? No, not likely. He'd been at several of the evening lectures, so there was something going on in his psyche. The thing was, as much as she cared about that aspect, she didn't care right now because she wanted what he offered.

Accepting it was a whole different thing.

"Because I can. Now, step closer and put your hand on me." He laughed lightly. "I promise I've had a shower."

She winced. A shower obviously hadn't been an issue for her before.

"Here, I'll make it easy on you." And he held out his hand.

She stared at it. It was just a hand. She'd shaken a man's hand before, hadn't she? A doctor or a lawyer, a cop's hand? She couldn't remember, but she must have.

She reached out and placed her hand in his. His fingers gently closed around hers, caging hers in. It didn't scare her. She tugged her fingers back experimentally, and he let her go. She took a deep breath. "Well, that wasn't so bad."

He chuckled. "Glad to hear it. Next?"

She shook her head. "I don't know."

"My hair, you said?"

He tilted his head, and like a moth to a flame, she couldn't resist the lure. She reached out to touch the silky, black waves. Short but with a hint of curl around his ears, his hair felt...normal. She laughed. "I don't know why I thought it would be anything else, but it feels normal."

He peered up at her from his odd position. "I would hope so."

She slipped her fingers through the waves, letting the curls wrap around her fingers. "It feels like a woman's hair."

"We do share similarities between the two sexes," he

mocked.

She smiled and continued to stroke her fingers through his hair. He shifted suddenly and she bolted backwards.

"Whoa, easy now. I was only changing my position a bit."

She took a deep, shaky breath. "You startled me."

"Yeah, I got that. But I'm not here to attack you. Remember that."

"Easy to remember on a mental level, but years of fear on a visceral level make it harder to control these reactions."

"That makes sense." He studied her for a moment. "If you want to continue this experiment…" and he waited for a response from her. She held her hand to her chest and gave a sharp nod. "…then I have a suggestion."

She stared at him and waited. "We'll go to my room so you can leave any time you want to, instead of worrying about how to get rid of me here, and I will lie down and you can touch me as you want to."

Her face flushed hot.

He cocked his head, a knowing look because of what had to be a chartreuse color on her face. "I wasn't really thinking you were ready for that kind of touching."

She shook her head frantically, but inside, her heart, mind, and hormones were screaming, "Yes!"

He stood up. "Come on. We don't have tons of time here, so let's do this."

Before she'd had time to process it, they were standing inside his room. He walked to the bed, pulled off his shirt, and dropped backwards on his bed. "Go for it."

THIS WAS GOING to kill him. What had possessed him to

put himself through this torture? Tinkerbelle was so damn attractive, but she was a bambina in the world of sex. She wanted to experience all the good stuff but had only been dished piles of shit so far in life. He'd love to be able to help her do this, but at the same time, he could hear his brother's voice in the background. "Dude, what has she got to do with your healing? You have a purpose there this week, and it doesn't include Tinkerbelle."

Except maybe it did.

As he lay there calmly, relaxed, waiting for her to get up the nerve to touch him, he realized he didn't know what the answer was for himself, but he wasn't stuffed full of rage at the moment. So that was an improvement.

Then he felt it.

Tinkerbelle's gossamer wing – okay, so not likely, but it was as gentle as that. He felt his stomach muscles bunching under her gentle fingertips. She slid them across his ribs gently, following the grooves and bumps of his torso that she could reach from her side of the bed. He'd have suggested she straddle him, but that would have sent her screaming. Too bad. The thought of her riding him was just about perfect. She'd have to be on top. As scared as she was, it would be the only way, at least the first time.

Once his mind started down that path, there was no stopping it. If he didn't watch it, she'd end up with an eyeful and this whole experiment would take a horrible turn. He worked hard at tensing his thigh muscle to keep his erection from getting any bigger. Realizing she'd stilled made him peek under his closed lid. She was watching his thigh. She had no idea what he was doing or why, but in true form, she was fascinated by his muscles. He groaned lightly. "I'm not sure how this experiment is going, but maybe you could say something. I feel very exposed here."

"Sorry," she said almost absentmindedly. "Is that why you are tightening and clenching your thigh?"

He debated answering her. How much trust could she take?

Then he decided that in a safe environment as she was in, maybe she needed to hear the truth.

"No," he said, and winced. "I'm trying to not let my sexual urges bring on a full erection. I doubt you're ready to see that. Or touch that…" he added humorously.

Silence, except for her heavy breathing. He opened his gaze to see her eyes locked on his face, as if scared to look anywhere else. Her breathing was shallow, not quite hyperventilating but close.

"It's okay. I'm fine. I am not about to lose control."

She swallowed again.

And the devil made him add, "But you could if you felt like it."

He didn't think her eyes could get any bigger, wider, and rounder, but damn it, they did. Immediately, he was sorry. "I'm just kidding. I'm feeling a little odd lying here like this, so my attempt at humor was just to ease my discomfort level."

She stepped back. "I'm sorry," she said instantly.

He didn't move, afraid she'd run. "Why?"

"You're uncomfortable." This time, she raised her puzzled gaze up at him. "I imagine it's demeaning. I'm sorry."

"It's not demeaning. You didn't ask. I offered. Big difference. Sorry my humor was off the mark. I'm fine. I'm just lying here. You've hardly touched me."

She took a step back, and he recognized the mood had been broken. "Okay, I'm going to sit up." She watched as he swung his legs around and sat on the edge of the bed. "Now, come closer. I want you to sit on my lap."

Her gaze shot up to meet his. "Yes, that's a normal request. You'll see lots of girls sitting on their guy's laps in a park, at a party, at any place and any time." He smiled engagingly. "It's a good experience." He opened his arms wide. "Just sit down."

She looked like she wanted to, but the fear and the uncertainty was keeping her at bay.

He opened his arms. "Come on, Tinkerbelle. Just sit down."

She winced. "I'm being an idiot, aren't I?"

"Yes," he said, delighted when a laugh was forced from her. She took a step and plunked her tiny butt on his left thigh. "Wow, don't you have any cushion on you?"

"Not much."

She bounced ever so slightly and then shook her head. "Damn rock. So not comfortable."

"Maybe, but look instead at what you've done," he pointed out quietly.

His breath was almost lifting her hair, she was so close. She turned to speak and realized they were almost eye level and her mouth was almost touching his. And she froze.

Then she did something that almost broke his heart.

She said in a small voice, barely above a whisper, "Can I touch you again? There's something I want to do."

His eyebrows shot up. He was curious but trying to stay calm enough to give her the courage she needed, so he nodded. "Absolutely."

Her eyes locked on his for a moment as if to make sure he was serious, then damn if she didn't lean in and place her lips against his in a Tinkerbelle of a kiss.

He was stunned. That this foray into touching could lead to something more intimate had obviously crossed his mind, but he hadn't expected it to. He hurt knowing what Tinkerbelle had been through, but like she said, it had been a long time ago. Maybe not so painful as it would have been if the attack had been recent, but still ready to ruin her life in so many ways. An insidious poison that attacked at odd times.

He had seen her come so far in such a short time, and he appreciated that a lot of what had been missing in her life was an opportunity to move forward. Somehow, he'd become that opportunity.

Had Jenna predicted this turn of events? Surely not.

And just what did he want to do with this new job role? The priority was for Tinkerbelle not to get hurt, and that meant what? Not physically hurt? Not emotionally hurt? Both?

Did he want to be her opportunity? His body tightened, and he groaned silently. Damn it. He was male. Of course he wanted to bed her. But there was no guarantee he'd be putting himself through anything but exquisite torture and no satisfaction, other than what he'd give himself at the end of the day.

But this wasn't about him, and it wasn't about getting something out of this. It was about Tinkerbelle.

He sat in the chair, his mind consumed with that brush of her lips on his, when she did it again.

He sighed and let his lips open.

She stilled.

"Nice," he murmured so as not to scare her.

He opened his eyes and watched hers get bigger, but inside, deep inside, was a hunger he knew well. A hunger for what she'd never had. A hunger for what she really wanted. A physical hunger for a simple, caring touch, a sexual hunger to explore her own needs and an emotional hunger to no longer be on the outside of a relationship.

A hunger for freedom from this huge issue in her life.

And damn if he didn't feel many of those same hungers, too.

Then she lowered her head and kissed him a third time.

CHAPTER 13

TANIA KNEW SHE shouldn't be doing this. For her sake, she wanted to continue forever because it felt wonderful, but she knew this had to be difficult for him. He didn't even know her, and here she was, using his body, his maleness, as some kind of educational toy. And damn if he wasn't perfect for the job.

With a sad sigh, she pulled back. "I should stop."

He kept his eyes closed, but his lips quirked. "Why? You haven't even started yet."

"Not fair, I kissed you."

"Ha," he mocked. "That wasn't a kiss."

She stared at him, curiosity in her eyes. Her mouth opened then closed again. As if unable to keep the words back, she said, "What's a kiss then?"

He opened his eyes and asked, "Do you not know?"

She flushed but faced him bravely. "Only what I've seen in movies or read in books."

"Romance books," he teased.

Her cheeks warmed. "Maybe."

"They aren't exactly realistic."

"True. But I already had a hefty dose of realism in my life, thank you." She stood up and walked to the window.

"Come on, sweetheart. I'm working really hard to not touch you and scare you away, so please don't let the odd comment do the same thing."

She turned around to study him. "Do you want to touch me?"

His eyebrows shot up and he snorted. "Of course."

She shook her head. "There's no 'of course' about it."

"Come here."

She took a tentative step forward, but indecision warred inside. Then she took another; in for a penny, in for a pound, or whatever the old saying was. If she was going to get anywhere, she had to step over these barriers. She walked closer until she stood in front of him. Slowly, he closed his knees, caging her in front of him. Her heart raced and she stared down at the tiny prison and stepped back. And he let her.

She took a shaky breath. "You know I can't stand to be held prisoner, right? Held down..." Her gaze bored into his, making sure he understood. "That force, that kind of strength and restraint will send me running..."

He opened his arms. "Sweetheart, have I done anything to cross the line?"

She shook her head.

"And I won't."

"How do I know that? What if you get angry, or sexually aroused..." she left that last bit hanging as once again her cheeks fired up.

"Meaning you think I'm likely to get so aroused that I'll rape you?"

There. It was out in the open. "No, I don't *think* you'd do that, but my mind and my body have a disconnect when it comes to this issue."

"Understood." His voice leveled off as if he fought some internal issue. "What exactly are we looking at here?"

She swallowed. "Pardon?"

"No, we're dancing around here, but let's lay it on the line. I'm a straight kind of guy. Are you wanting to have sex?" His gaze pinned her in place, delving deeper into her mind until she felt his presence inside. So deep inside, she swore he was in her body already.

"What I want and what I can do are two different things."

"So let's start with what you want."

"I want it all. I want sex, to enjoy sex, to be able to please my partner during sex."

The words slipped out so fast – there was no holding back with this man. She didn't know how it happened, but she was starting to care for him, maybe because he was being so gentle with her.

"And now the 'what can you do' part," he said.

She waved her hand at him. "Only what we've been do-ing."

"Except that yesterday, this morning even, you would have said this wasn't something you could do because it hadn't happened yet. Now if we go a little further, it will put what you can do closer in line with what you want to do."

"A little further?" she swallowed hard. "Like how much further?"

HE DIDN'T KNOW if he was using the right tactic, but it seemed important for her to push her line back a little further. She'd come a huge distance already, and if he was to list all of the first steps she'd taken today, it would probably surprise her – possibly scare her. So far, she'd done all the touching; he'd just been a male form for her to test her gossamer wings on. He was so much more, but she wasn't ready to see it, and maybe he wasn't ready to offer it.

He had no problems initiating her into lovemaking. He'd rather that than straight sex, and whether she understood it or not, she couldn't go through this process without having some feelings for the person she'd shared the journey with.

Was she prepared for that? Or would her own emotional overload not allow her to recognize it for a long time? He admired what she was trying to do. Understood the need in so many ways. And could see himself caring for her – deeply. What a quagmire. If he did want to pursue this and she wasn't able to take these next steps, was he prepared to stick around when sex wasn't going to be part of the equation? At least, not for a long time? He was no fool. Nor was he a teenager. He'd been married. He had loved and been loved, but there was no doubt a healthy, happy sex life had enhanced their relationship. To think of one without a sexual element…well, if he was honest, he wasn't sure he could do it.

And that didn't make him feel good. He was a sexual male in his prime, but he was starting to wonder if he wasn't still an immature male emotionally. How did one mature in that way – if it wasn't through moments like this? Through strife and pain. Well, he'd had a lot of pain…had he grown from it, or had he become stuck in his anger, unwilling to move past it?

Damn Jenna after all.

Maybe he was exactly where he needed to be, helping Tania resolve her demons. In the very act of helping her deal with her demons, he just might find that his only existed because he'd been keeping them alive.

Because it was easier.

It was easier because then he wouldn't have to trust anyone again.

And therefore couldn't be hurt at the level his ex-wife had gutted him.

If he ever needed proof of courage and need to trust, he only had to look at Tania. She'd already made bigger steps than he had in a direction he couldn't imagine having to deal with. And he'd been sitting inside his petty corner, refusing to come out because of someone who was no longer in his life.

What the hell?

How and when had he given away his power – and to her, his ex-wife – of all people?

Then he looked at Tania. Sure, she'd had more years to get over her trauma than he'd had, but since it had been such a physical violation, she had so many other issues to deal with.

And look at how well she was stepping up to the plate.

How could he do any less?

CHAPTER 14

TANIA COULD BARELY breathe, waiting for his answer. An answer she received in the form of a half-smile. "In the spirit of cooperation and experimentation, what would be the next step you'd like to take?"

She frowned, looked away, and then glanced back at him. She gave him a little smile. "You could kiss me."

He grinned. "My pleasure." He stood up until he towered over her. Her gaze widened in shock and she swallowed. "Uhm, that's not going to work."

His grin widened. In a sudden move, he flipped her so she was standing on the bed looking down at him. She shrieked.

Surprised at the suddenness of the movement, she reached out and put her hands on his shoulders for stability.

"This isn't going to work, either." She shook her head. "You're too tall."

Kane shook his head at her innocence. He sat down and patted his knee. "Then you'd better sit back down again."

She frowned, jumped off the bed, and sat down again.

At his smirk, she glared. "What's so funny?"

"You. You let me pick you up, turn you around, and you willingly grabbed onto me to stop yourself from falling. Now you're back sitting on my knee. See what you've become accustomed to so quickly?"

Her mind turned his comment upside and downside as she realized he was correct. She hadn't flinched when he'd lifted her. She had shrieked instead, but it wasn't due to fear.

Not from him.

"I'm not scared of you," she said, wonder in her voice. "You're big enough to squash me flat without thinking about it, but you wouldn't. At least, not to me. At least not right now."

"Never." He slid his hand up her slender back – gently, soft, indomitable. When he reached her neck, he squeezed ever so slightly and nudged her head forward. "Kiss me."

"I thought you were going to kiss me instead."

Their eyes met, locked, and heat coursed through her. She wanted to kiss him – wanted his lips on hers, wanted to feel whatever he could make her feel. His mouth so close to her own, his breath mingled with hers when he whispered, "Kiss me."

His words washed over her as her eyes drifted closed and she leaned in, placing her lips on his.

Instantly, the hand behind her head gentled and his lips moved on hers, taking a taste of her like he hadn't before. He brushed his lips back and forth, his tongue sliding across her sensitized skin.

"Open for me."

The words filtered through the haze in her mind, tugging at her to understand them – but she didn't want to. She pressed her lips harder against his. He slipped his tongue out. Her mouth blossomed under his, taking, sharing, needing as much as he gave her. She followed his lead and gave back every bit of the pleasure he was giving her.

She lost track of time…of place…of purpose. There was only one thing in her world right now – Kane's mouth.

His tongue stroked, teased, and tasted. She sighed and sagged against him.

He trailed kisses down the side of her cheek, to her ear, and down the nape of her neck. She shivered, shifting to give him better access. He could have anything he wanted as long as he kept this up. In the background, someone was moaning, a sound that excited her almost as much as Kane's seductive touch. Then she realized the moans were hers.

And then she recognized something else – her arms were wrapped around his neck and she no longer sat on his knee. Instead, she was curled sideways in his lap.

She shifted slightly to look up into his face as he lowered his head and dropped a soul-stealing kiss on her.

She melted.

"You are lethal," she whispered when she could.

"Not me, you. Us. Together. Soooo…good."

He lowered his head again.

And she met him halfway. In fact, she was dying to taste him. After a lifetime of doing without and living with the fear of never getting to experience this and having someone here with her, having someone who was willing to let her experiment and had the advantage of being seriously hot felt so very good – she was a dying woman lost in a cloud of sensuality.

She wished it could go on forever.

He pulled back slightly. She whimpered and tried to tug him back down toward her. When he didn't budge, she opened her eyes slowly, loving the look in his eyes, like he was enjoying himself with someone he cared about. Such an addictive look.

"Hey," she whispered. Not wanting to move, she rested her head against his shoulder.

"Hey, yourself." He dropped a kiss on her forehead. "How are you doing?"

"Better than okay. Good thing I didn't discover kissing when I was in high school – I'd never have shown up for class."

Laughter rumbled through his chest. "I had that exact same problem."

"Ha! I'm surprised anyone goes at all if they understand this is an option."

"Which is why mothers don't want their daughters to find out too early."

"And why guys can't get enough?" She grinned, her bones relaxed, her mind empty, just enjoying the moment. And she wished she could stay like this.

He wrapped his arms around her and hugged her close. She froze at the unexpected movement then relaxed.

"Okay?"

"Okay, but I think that might have been a hug. Not sure as I haven't experienced a lot of them in my life." And she hadn't in many years. Her mother and sisters weren't demonstrative, not cold, just not the touchy feely kind of people. She was now wondering if Kane was. She'd loved her father dearly, but she hadn't been able to be around him for a long time. The strain had destroyed her parents' marriage. He'd stayed close for a long time but had been transferred back East years ago. She'd told him to go. It was better this way, knowing he was hoping for more and she had no more to give…

She hadn't finished speaking when she was engulfed in another hug, but there was no fear.

He eased his arms back. "There, a hug. Although they are even better when standing up."

At his comment, her eyes popped open and she was already bouncing to her feet.

Laughing, he stood and wrapped his arms around her in a gentle hug.

And they stayed like that for a long time.

Until Tania's phone went off.

KANE HATED WHEN technology intruded. Tania reached for her phone, saw she had a text, and gasped. "Oh, no. We're late for dinner."

"Really?" Kane reached for his own phone and whistled long and low. "Okay, I had no idea it was so late." In fact, hours appeared to have disappeared on them. "Let's go before we miss out entirely."

He walked toward the door only to realize she wasn't following. "Tania?"

"I'm coming. I just…" Tania sighed. "I just don't want them all to know."

"Know what?" He glanced at his watch, ushered her out the door, and locked it behind him. "We're supposed to be working on our project. So we worked a little late. No one is going to know anything unless you say so."

"I've never been any good at lying," she muttered.

"No need to lie. We haven't been doing anything wrong." He opened the stairway doors. "Act natural. No one is staring at us. No one cares. Remember that."

When she didn't answer, he turned to look behind him to make sure she was following. She was, but a worried look had taken over her features. "Okay."

He grinned. "If you walk in like that, it's going to look like we're guilty of something."

She smirked. "I guess we are, in a way."

At the next landing, he opened the door and stepped into the main floor where the restaurant was. "And in what way is that?"

"We didn't do our homework."

They walked into the restaurant laughing and smiling. The others noticed, but no one made a comment.

Just like he'd expected.

CHAPTER 15

D INNER WAS SIMPLE, fast, and silent, at least on Tania's part. She smiled brightly at everyone, and when her food arrived, she tucked into it with a ravenous hunger.

"You must have worked up an appetite." Robin poked fun at her as she finished her own pasta.

Tania nodded as she forked up another mouthful of salad to avoid having to answer. Before she was halfway done, several of the other members of the group were getting up and drifting away. Good.

She settled back to enjoy the rest of her meal. By the time she was done, the table had mostly emptied. She smiled and ordered coffee.

"Tania, how was your day?" Jenna shifted from her seat at the far end of the table to one across from Tania. Robin chose that moment to excuse herself, leaving Jenna and Tania essentially alone. Kane was finishing his meal on the opposite side of the table.

The coffee arrived just then, giving Tania a moment to collect her thoughts.

"So, was it a good day?"

"Absolutely." She sat back and rubbed her tummy. "That filled a hole." Forestalling any attempt on Jenna's part to get too personal, she asked, "What's on the schedule for tomorrow?"

Jenna smiled at the change in topic and launched into the plans for the middle of the seminar. Realizing she'd skated by, Tania devoted the next half hour to discussing the rest of the seminar. Jenna had lots of work for them. In fact, as Jenna handed over a few sheets, Tania realized they'd missed the handout she'd given out before the group had ordered dinner. It looked like there was homework tonight.

Damn. She'd been hoping to spend time with Kane. Speaking of which, she lifted her head from her papers and looked around the room, but there was no sign of him. She did not notice when he'd left, but she'd studiously kept her focus off him so as to not draw attention to their relationship.

She wondered if he had the homework. The thought of having an excuse to see him again tonight made her toes curl. She tried hard to keep a straight face. The last thing she wanted was for Jenna to pick up on the attraction. Then she caught Jenna's eye and recognized it was too damn late. Jenna already knew.

Lifting her cup to her lips, she drained her mug then pushed her chair back. "I'll say good night then, see if Robin wants to work on this together." With a quick smile at Jenna, she walked away.

And damned if she didn't feel Jenna's concerned gaze as she escaped.

She texted Robin out in the lobby and asked if she wanted to work on the homework together, only to find out that Robin had done hers.

Double damn. Stay alone in her room or go somewhere to do it? She chose the pub attached to the hotel. She could grab a beer, sit down at a table, and work her way through the information.

How hard could it be?

Ten minutes later, she was sitting at a window table watching the sun's rays march across the horizon. Vancouver was a beautiful city, and the university campus was even more stunning. Sipping her beer, she started on the homework.

And cringed. The homework was a worksheet on their yet-to-be-seriously-started project. There was a place to list the theme, objective, and process. The project sheet was starting to read like a damn lab report.

Crap. This was definitely an assignment to do together. She brightened. A great excuse to see him again.

Which brought her full circle. Should she be spending so much time with him? Was it a good idea? She knew falling for him probably wasn't, but it was a little too late for that.

The man was hot, kissed like a dream, and photographed even better.

Where could she go wrong with such a choice?

While she sat there grinning, someone stepped up beside her. "Hey lady, want some company?"

And before she had a chance to answer, a young male slid into the seat across from her at the table.

"No, thanks," she said politely. "I'm working."

"No, you're not." He snagged the paper from her hand and tossed it beside him. "You're too pretty to care about stuff like that. Why don't we go find a room and see if we can't find something more fun to do together?"

Tania hated drunks and aggressive males, and worse, she hated being in a position where she had to deal with them. She had over half a beer left. She glanced around the room, wondering if there was a spot up by the bar. At least there, the bartender was likely to chase off anyone bothering her.

She hadn't made it through this many years of university without seeing her fair share of drunken guys. But the man sitting across from her wasn't drunk enough to be at the pass-out stage. He looked to be just in the rosy glow of a couple of beers. Not too bad yet, depending on what kind of drunk he was.

She gave him a firm "No, thanks," and stood up.

He stood up, too, and leaned forward. "What's the matter, beauty queen? Am I not good enough for you? Well, I got news for you. I'm better than you, you fucking bitch." By now, his voice had risen to the point of attracting attention. Just why did it never bring help?

Bitterness clogged her throat. She'd learned a long time ago that people preferred to stay out of things rather than get into trouble helping someone else.

"Look, I just want to have a beer in peace and do my homework."

"Ha. Homework. You're nothing but a stuck-up bitch that thinks you're better than everyone else. Another of the uni bitches who hand it out to everyone but the working man."

She glanced around to find some guys watching with big grins on their faces. A few frowned into their beers but were trying to ignore the scenario. A couple of women standing by the door got up and left, and that was about the only avenue left to her.

She picked up her glass, guzzled back the beer, placed it on the table, snatched up her homework, and turned to leave.

He grabbed her arm. Inside, her nerves knotted and her pulse started to race. She jerked her arm back. "Don't touch me."

"Don't touch you or what?" he sneered. "I've seen stuck-up bitches like you before. You're all prissy-white on the outside but you're just another fucking cunt looking for a man between your legs."

She could feel his words like small darts hitting her on some visceral level. She hated it when guys did this, used a few beers to loosen their mouths so they could say whatever the hell they wanted. She backed up and tried to navigate a way through the full room. She just wanted to get to her room safely and alone. So much for the quiet drink idea.

She'd almost reached the exit of the pub when she heard something behind her. She spun around, and instinct and training had her immediately shifting to a slight crouch to assess the danger.

And damn if it wasn't the same guy. He stumbled forward. Another guy shoved him into an empty seat. "Leave her alone."

"What the fuck." Arms flailing, the drunk managed to stand up and resume his way to the exit. "I just want to go home."

Tania slipped through the door into the hotel lobby and waited off to one side.

The drunk came out and stopped. He straightened and looked around. He wasn't as drunk as she'd hoped. He'd had the presence of mind to fake it with the other man.

Sitting in the lobby, she was relatively safe. Hotel security would help her if the man got out of line. Better a minor drunk than a full-scale attack. She wasn't twelve anymore walking home from school, innocent in the way of the world and men. The man made his way to the front door of the hotel, and she relaxed. He was leaving, so there was nothing to worry about after all. Except the incident had left a bad taste in her mouth. She wanted to rest in the security of her room, maybe have a bath, and get through her homework. And a decent night's sleep would be good.

She walked to the wall of elevators and pushed the button to bring one to the lobby.

When the door opened, several people stepped off. She stepped on.

Just as the door closed, another man raced in.

The drunk.

Tania stumbled to the front corner of the elevator. She'd already pressed the close door button and wished she could open it again. She pressed it again several times. She'd take the stairs over an altercation any day, but the drunk zeroed in on her.

He stared at her, anger growing deep in his murky gaze. "Bitch. Think you're too good for me."

His fingers flexed. Tania risked a quick glance at the light above the moving elevator. It was almost time to get off, but she had to get around him. If there were other guests waiting to get on, that would be helpful.

Just then, the floor dinged and the double doors opened. She raced out, but he grabbed her shirt as she made her escape and dragged her backwards. She spun around and jammed her elbow into his throat. He roared and released her.

She desperately wanted the safety of her room, but she didn't want him to know where she was staying.

"Goddamn it. Get the fuck back here." She was already racing down the hallway, only he was faster and caught her just outside her room. He grabbed her and slammed her up against the wall. She cried out but kept her head. She rammed her elbow into his gut, stomped on his instep, then turned and shoved both fists upward into his chin before she brought them both down on the back of his head as he doubled over. She spun around and bolted.

Into a mountain of spitting fury.

Kane.

KANE THOUGHT HE'D heard Tania's cry outside the door. He'd raced into the hallway in time to see Tinkerbelle slam, stomp, and then give a doozy of a double-fisted blow to some guy's nose.

Blood was spurting between the guy's fingers even as he swayed to stay on his feet.

Then Tinkerbelle slammed into him. He grabbed her by the waist and lifted her to his eye level. She kicked out wildly, crying out in panic until she realized who held her. She hung suspended in his arms, gasping for breath. Then groaned, closed her eyes, and sagged in place.

"Are you okay?" he asked.

She opened her eyes to stare at him, stunned.

He gave her a little shake. "Damn it, Tania, talk to me. Did this asshole hurt you?"

She gasped and shook her head. "No. No, he tried…I hit him. I think I hit him." She kept shaking her head, only now the shakes were working their way down her tiny frame.

He lowered her to the floor, shoved her behind him, and eyed the asshole standing in front of him.

Some of the alcoholic haze was leaving his eyes as pain replaced it. He had both hands clasped over his face. He looked at Kane, then at Tania, then back at Kane. "I think she broke my nose." He blinked at the two of them, and then said to Tania, "Why did you break my nose?"

Kane snorted. "You think I'm going to let you get away with blaming her? You're twice Tinkerbelle's size. Do you think you can attack a woman and get away with it?"

The drunk looked at him. "She attacked me," he said in a nasal voice. "She broke my nose."

"I defended myself. You attacked me," Tania cried. "At the pub verbally, then when I didn't like your suggestion, in the elevator."

Kane's fists clenched. Tinkerbelle was tiny. She was always going to have to watch out for predators. At least she'd taken some self-defense training. The world was full of assholes like this one.

Hotel security came running up the stairs, then quickly surrounded the two men. "What's the problem here?"

Kane pointed at the drunk looking closer to collapsing now, but whether that was from the drinking or the blood loss, he didn't know. Or care. "This guy attacked a woman."

"Did not."

Kane was surprised that Tania didn't immediately pipe up with 'did, too', as that was what he'd have expected. But she stayed quiet.

"I was minding my own business," he squeaked out, "when Tinkerbelle attacked me."

The hotel security guys looked at him and sighed. "Tinkerbelle?"

The drunk nodded rapidly. "She broke my nose." One security guard led the drunk to the elevator. "Let's get that nose taken care of."

"She broke it. Tinkerbelle broke it."

"Right, buddy. Sure she did. And how much have you had to drink tonight?"

The second security guard spoke through a device on his

shoulder strap, letting the others know what was going on and preparing for the drunk to be received on the main floor. He turned to Kane. "Sir, did you hit him?"

Kane snorted and gave a hard smirk. "Nah, do you think I'd have broken his nose? I'd have cracked that asshole's head wide open if I had the chance. Still will if he comes back."

"And his story about Tinkerbelle?" The security guard shook his head as if to say he'd seen it all.

Kane laughed and stepped to one side. "Meet Tania, also known as Tinkerbelle."

Tania lifted her hand in a small finger wave. "Hi."

CHAPTER 16

TANIA HAD TRIED to brush off the incident as minor, but neither the hotel security nor Kane would allow her to.

"He's made trouble here before. We have to take an incident report and contact the police. If we don't, he'll just come back and do it again."

The security man looked at her. "Consider if he were to do that next time to a girl who didn't know any self-defense techniques."

She sat back because of course, that had been her twelve years ago. Her attack hadn't been his first offense, either. He'd told her at the time that he'd done this before, but he preferred children; they couldn't get their stories listened to anyhow.

The reminder hurt, plus it made her responsibilities clear. She had to do this for the next woman's sake.

With Kane at her side, they went down to the lobby and she made a statement before she repeated the process with the police. Talk about overkill, but the men were adamant.

When it was over, she was drained.

They'd been drinking coffee during the whole ordeal, and now she was so wired she wasn't sure she could sleep.

After the day she had, she just wanted to not dream.

Hours later, alone, Kane had left her at her doorway after making sure she was okay. With a gentle but distant kiss goodnight, she made her way to her bed.

The nightmares hit a couple of hours later. Tania woke in a cold sweat, whimpering in her sleep as she felt the rough hand over her mouth, the ripping of her clothing, the male body swamping her, overwhelming her, and the never-to-be-forgotten feeling of being raped.

She lay there dry-eyed for a long time. When the memories faded back slightly, she got up and filled a glass with water. She walked around her room sipping the cold drink. She pulled her nightdress away from her clammy skin, hating that after so long, the memories could still overwhelm her. Still ruin a good night's sleep, take this rational, balanced woman and turn her into a bag of nerves.

She understood that the drunkard's attack had precipitated the nightmares always lurking behind the scenes to destroy her calm. Even though she understood, it didn't change the fact that it still happened, that nothing she did stopped the nightmares for good.

It had been months, if not years, since her last really bad nightmare. She couldn't remember what had set those off. Exhausted, she sat back down on her bed and flopped backwards. She didn't know how to go back to sleep. She'd brought melatonin with her, but taking it often left her groggy in the morning. She sat up and ran through several yoga moves to release some of the tension, but that just brought up images of Kane. He'd been wonderfully protective, almost irritatingly so, demanding she file a report and deliciously sweet with his goodnight kiss. She wanted so much more.

And she was a mess with nothing but a broken shell to offer.

She'd come so far and yet not far enough.

Immediately, a protest jumped into her mind. She'd come a hell of a long way. She'd fought off her attacker, survived to see him taken away, and so what if she had a nightmare or two? Surely that was normal. She might not be whole, but it didn't mean she was so far gone she couldn't heal. It was – she'd just proven it.

And she'd keep on proving it.

But her one chance to get through a sexual encounter was with Kane.

Even her wording made her wince. Who'd want anything to do with that? Lovemaking? Yes. Getting through a sexual encounter? Nasty.

She could almost hear Jenna saying the terminology was important. It showed she was still distancing herself from the personal element of lovemaking. A sexual encounter was cold, clinical, like a lab experiment. She almost laughed. Wouldn't Kane love that description?

And then she remembered those arms around her, his lips moving on hers, his tongue…there was nothing cold about Kane, nothing clinical about what they'd done that afternoon. She glanced at the clock. Okay, yesterday afternoon.

Even now, her body warmed at the thought of those hands of his. How gently he'd held her. How his strength had been so controlled. She couldn't imagine what it would take for a man like that to lose control. He'd be a force to contend with. He had problems with women. She'd heard it a couple of times in his voice, saw the look in his eyes when he watched couples walk by. He'd been hurt. How he'd managed the hurt was the problem. She wished he'd talked to her, but he didn't trust her. Maybe that was the problem. Trust. She didn't trust any man not to hurt her again physically, and maybe he didn't trust any woman to not hurt him emotionally. Someone in his life had ripped a hole in his body, creating so much damage he'd been forced into therapy to try and heal himself.

Maybe for his career. Another woman? To stop his brother from pushing? Who knew what was the driving force going on in there, but he was here. And he was dealing. She didn't know how this project was supposed to help him, but it was testing her.

She sighed and realized if she wasn't going to sleep, she might as well finish her homework.

Tucked in bed, she came back to the first question – the theme of their project. She'd considered light and dark, but it wasn't quite right. She wrestled with it for a few moments then moved on to the next question. This one was easier as it was about process. She got to work.

A half hour later and she was done mentally, but she hadn't gotten even halfway on the homework. But maybe she was ready to try to sleep.

Closing her light, she crawled into bed and relaxed.

Then it hit her. The theme. Was her idea right? Could it work? She thought about the images she'd taken. The look in Kane's eyes, the changes from one day to the next. She hadn't even downloaded today's images, and she needed to. It would tell her if she was on the right track.

The theme – skin.

KANE WOKE THE next morning and immediately got angry all over again. He'd been so proud of Tania and her moves and pissed off at the drunk. Even more so when he understood this wasn't an isolated incident; this guy was a hell of an ugly drunk, and research would likely show he was a controlled, angry man who, when under the influence of alcohol, found it much harder to control the rage that lived just under his skin. And he felt empowered to let it out and be the angry man who lived inside. Kane wanted the guy stopped before he really hurt someone. That it could have been his Tinkerbelle last night scared him shitless.

That he considered Tinkerbelle his terrified him even more.

What the hell?

He didn't come here for that.

Sex was one thing…this was something else altogether. The trouble is, he didn't know what. She was…broken…to use her words. He had his own problems. The last thing he should be doing was hooking up with someone who wasn't whole. He winced. But he wasn't whole himself – who was he to expect someone not dealing with major trauma issues to be looking at him?

Then he wasn't looking for himself. It's the last thing he wanted.

But Tinkerbelle was…different.

But she was still female, so how different could she be?

Very, he knew. Her experiences had molded who she was. She didn't have the deviousness of other women he knew. But he could be wrong. He'd been horribly wrong at the time when it had counted, and he didn't want to go through that ever again.

He showered, dressed, and headed down to breakfast. He was early, but maybe he could check in with security to see what had happened last night. The drunk had been spouting off something about suing Tinkerbelle, but he hadn't been able to describe her nor name her correctly.

Kane hoped in the cold light of day that the man had come to his senses. Kane would push for him to be charged with assault if he could, but that decision wasn't his to make and if it came down to Tinkerbelle pressing charges, he figured she'd just want it all to go away.

He'd wanted to ask her about her rapist. Had he been found? Charged? Done his time and been released? But he figured she'd tell him if she wanted to. It didn't stop him from wanting the details, though. He could put a call out to a buddy if he wanted to bad enough. He could get the details, but it seemed underhanded prying into her life, a life he'd been allowed to see just one corner of. A good corner, but still just a corner.

He'd be the first to admit he wanted into every corner.

He couldn't find the security guards, so he left a message for them to contact him later. Then he headed into the restaurant for breakfast where he found Jenna waiting alone at the table.

"Kane." She smiled up at him. "I was hoping for a chance to see you alone. What on Earth happened last night?"

He winced. "It might be better if you asked Tania, but as it involved security and police, I can give you the short and dirty version."

He explained, watching her face drain of color. "She handled herself well." He grinned, pride in his voice. "Actually, she handled herself really well."

"Well." Jenna shook her head slowly, letting out a gust of air. "Poor Tania. What a difficult thing for any woman."

"True. But it was also a win for her. After all she's been through, she wasn't a victim this time. She was the victor."

Jenna studied his face. "She told you?"

He nodded and smiled up at the waitress who'd arrived with the coffee pot. After she'd left, he turned his attention back to Jenna. "Yes, she did."

"Interesting."

"In what way?" God, he hated how Jenna said that word so often. He hated feeling like there was more going on here than he understood. Of course, there was – there always was – but he didn't want it to be a constant irritation in the back of his mind.

He waited for Jenna to answer.

"I'm just surprised she told you about her history."

"We're working on this project together, isn't it normal for her to have shared something like that?"

Jenna's lips quirked.

Okay, so that came across as slightly defensive. Damn.

"It's intensely personal." Jenna studied him closely.

He frowned. He should have seen that coming. "And…"

"Nothing. I'm happy she was comfortable enough to share with you."

He frowned at her, saw the twinkling in her eyes, and understood she was poking at him to see what might come out. He smirked. "It's early, professor, but not so early that you're going to get anything out of me."

"Oh, so there is something to get, though, is there?"

He glared at her, and damn if her laughter didn't ripple free.

He sighed and lifted his coffee cup. No doubt about it, he had it bad.

Chapter 17

TANIA DRAGGED HERSELF into the restaurant, wishing she could just go back to bed. She had a headache, and her elbow hurt after defending herself last night.

The table was full. She caught Kane's gaze, and damn if her heart didn't speed up at the possibilities promised in his eyes. He'd turn any woman to mush. Oddly enough, not one of the other females at the table appeared to be bothered, but there were several others in the restaurant checking him out. His size alone attracted attention. That his voice was deep, dark, and promised midnight dreams helped a lot.

She sighed. Talk about being lovesick. Or was it lust struck? Stupid body. It could have stood up and sang hallelujah when she was high school. She'd have enjoyed spending time in the back seat of cars making out, especially if the guys kissed like Kane. Then again, how many guys could make her melt like he had?

Tired, she took the last empty seat and caught the waitress's eye, motioning desperately for coffee. It had been a long night, and getting through the morning meant she'd need some serious fortification. With that in mind, she ordered a big breakfast. She might be short and small, but her appetite was seriously large. Her breakfast, when it came, made her sigh with happiness.

"Whoa, isn't that a bit too much food for you?" asked

Robin, who was sitting across from her. Tania shrugged. "I'll let you know in twenty minutes."

"What did you do, work out all night?" Snide jokes started up. She ignored them all and plowed through her meal. When she laid her fork down, she was surprised to see she'd cleaned her plate.

She reached for the last piece of toast and polished it off, too.

When she raised her gaze, it was to see everyone staring at her. She raised an eyebrow in question. Kane asked in a gentle, humorous voice, "Would you like seconds?"

She smirked. "I'm good until lunch, thanks."

Jenna picked up the conversation from there, after which, they moved to the seminar room and got started on the homework.

"Tania, did you get a chance to do the homework?" Jenna asked.

"In the middle of the night when I couldn't sleep, I worked on it." She sighed. "But is it done? No."

"Sorry about all the trouble you had. I hope you're happy with the way the hotel dealt with the issue."

She nodded. "They were fine." She really didn't want to go into the whole mess again, but several people were looking at her oddly. She said, "Some drunk accosted me outside my room last night."

The women cried out. The men stayed silent.

After a quick explanation of what happened after that, she ended with, "As a result, I didn't get much sleep."

"I bet," Robin said with feeling. "Take it easy today."

"Sure. I'll be fine."

"Are you fine?" Jenna asked seriously. "Why don't we go for a walk outside and we'll talk?"

It was on the tip of her tongue to say she didn't need to, but the truth of the matter was her nightmares had returned with a vengeance. If she could figure out how to get her subconscious to let this all go, her nights would be much better. And talking about it just might be the answer.

"Sure." She stood up from the table and handed her homework to Kane. "I'll work on this when I get back."

He nodded. "I haven't even looked at it yet. Go. Enjoy your talk."

"Thanks." As she turned away, he added, "You look tired."

"I am. The nightmares were bad again last night." She walked outside with Jenna.

KANE WATCHED THE two women leave. One was small and normally walked with determination and focus, but today it looked like taking every step was hard work. Tall, stately Jenna strolled easily alongside Tania; they made a striking pair. He sat back down and looked at the homework sheets, but his mind returned to Tania's comment. Why hadn't he considered she'd have nightmares? Of course she would have them. That attack had to trigger bad memories, and when did those memories usually hit the hardest? During the dream state.

Damn.

He'd never even thought of it, so he'd gone to bed and slept like a baby while she'd barely gotten any rest. He could have helped her. He didn't know how, but he could have slept in the chair to watch over her. Then again, she might have found that even more disturbing. It's not like she'd ever slept with a man – innocently or not.

But he could have done something. Instead, he'd given her a gentle kiss and pushed her into her room with orders to lock the door.

Then his eye caught the theme question on Tania's page and the one word she'd written beside it. Skin. What the hell did that mean?

CHAPTER 18

THE FRESH BREEZE blew Tania's hair across her face as they exited the hotel's front doors. It was a beautiful day; even the breeze was warm. It was also early enough that the morning sunshine was fresh and bright and missing the muggy heat promised for later in the day.

"What were the nightmares about?"

Tania gave a broken laugh. "The rape. It's the same as always, triggered, no doubt, by last night's attack."

"Were you hurt last night? How bad was the attack?"

"Not bad in some ways, but bad enough." Tania shrugged. How did one determine how bad something was? "I was scared, but he didn't physically hurt me. I hurt him. I broke his nose, apparently." The reminder put a smile back on her face.

"Good. He deserved it."

"The police hauled him away, but I don't know the final story."

"I hope he's gone and stays gone. You don't need that around."

"No. I need sleep at this point."

"Do you want to miss the morning session and go back to your room?"

As tempting as that thought was, she didn't want to miss any time with Kane or the seminar. She was here for a reason and wanted to get as much out of this as she could. "No. I'll stay. I would like to stop the nightmares, though."

"Then lead me through the details. Let's see if we can find out what your subconscious was working on."

It took several minutes to relay the details as she remembered them. "I don't think there was anything new in these ones, just the same old, same old."

"But not as potent? You didn't wake up screaming?"

"No, not at all." Tania recognized the truth with surprise. "It was uncomfortable and I woke up in a cold sweat, but it wasn't nearly as bad."

"Good. Great, actually. When you think about it, last night's attack might have been a gift in that it gave you a chance to see where your subconscious thoughts are at. And it looks like they are slowly getting better."

"That's one way to look at it." She hadn't mentioned any of the intimate time she'd spent with Kane. It felt odd, almost disloyal to mention him in context of her healing to Jenna. Still, he might have had an impact on that same subconscious. As she thought about the problem, she realized Jenna was correct.

She was healing.

KANE TRIED TO single out Tania yet again to ask her about the homework. He wasn't sure where the hell she was going with that theme. He just knew he didn't want this to be a sex project. There was no way he wanted their relationship documented, and although she was here to heal, he didn't want his participation anywhere on paper. As long as she understood then he was good, otherwise…he was done with this assignment. She'd been sitting at the far end of the room after coming back with Jenna. He was surprised at feeling miffed that she hadn't come up to sit beside him. He wanted her to. He'd waited for her, had even saved her a seat. They were partners, damn it.

And she'd sat at the back of the class by the door. A half hour later when he checked, it was to see her empty seat. He glanced around the room, but there was no sign of her.

He frowned at the table. Given how tired she was, what was the chance that she'd gone to lie down? He continued to check on her empty seat until they broke for lunch. Rather than follow the group into the restaurant, he strode upstairs to her room and knocked quietly.

She opened the door. Her face lit up when she saw him. "Hey." She covered her mouth with the back of her hand as she yawned. "I just woke up."

"Ah. I wondered." He couldn't help but notice the sexy, tousled look she wore. "I was checking to make sure you're okay and had no ill effects from last night."

She smiled and pushed her dark blonde hair off her face. "No ill effects. Nightmares kept me awake, but as they weren't as bad as they have been in the past, I'll take that as a good sign."

"Are you ready to eat again then?" he teased. "It's lunch break now."

Her gaze widened. "I was going to have a quick shower, but lunch would be good." She considered it. "Give me a couple of minutes to get dressed again, and I'll walk down with you."

"Perfect."

Then to his surprise, she opened her door wider to let him in.

"You might as well come in and wait."

Damn if he was going to turn that down.

CHAPTER 19

TANIA SURPRISED HERSELF by inviting him in. There had been no need. He could have stayed out in the hallway for those few minutes. She bustled about grabbing her clothes, throwing the bedding back into position. With an embarrassed smile, she disappeared into the bathroom.

"Remember to be quick," he said.

"Be right back out."

In the bathroom, she reminded herself: Small steps, small steps. Well, she'd certainly been taking lots of small steps. Inviting him in was yet another one. Realizing the time was wasting as she stared in the mirror with a silly grin on her face, she dressed quickly and washed her face.

She opened the door and said, "Ready."

"Good, let's go." He walked out and turned to wait for her to follow. She closed and locked her door and almost ran into Robin. "Hey, I was just coming to check up on you."

Tania smiled. "Thanks. Kane here dragged me out of my room to make sure I don't starve."

"Ha. After your huge breakfast, you shouldn't need to eat again for a week." Her gaze wandered from Kane to Tania and back again speculatively.

Tania refused to let the heat rising swamp her cheeks. She walked towards the stairs – no more elevators for her – and called back, "I'm always hungry." She laughed and ran down the first flight. She had turned around the railing to start down the second when Kane passed her. He jumped.

"Hey, that's cheating," she called after his retreating back. She figured from the laughter floating upward that he wasn't bothered about any imaginary rules. He waited for her at the bottom of the stairs.

"Besides, your legs are longer."

He snorted. "So what? Pick yours up a little faster and you'd have made it."

"I doubt it." They walked into the restaurant and grabbed a quick meal as the laughter and joking continued. She'd never experienced anything like this relationship between a man and a woman. She loved it.

The afternoon session sent them off to work on their project. She ran back to her room, snagged her camera, and raced back down. Kane waited outside the front door for her.

After the heavy emotions of last night and the sense of freedom this morning, today's photo shoot couldn't be anything less than amazing. Life was just about perfect. Okay…maybe it was Kane who was perfect.

She walked beside him and said, "Where to?"

"I'm still not at home and still can't renovate my bathroom or do my yard work, so that leaves the touristy side."

"Sounds good."

"And then as someone took up much of my yesterday, I didn't get my workout in, so I will need to go to the fitness room sometime today."

"Perfect," she said, beaming. It was perfect. There were still some shots she wanted of him pushing his body. And for all she knew, he had different moves, new ones that would give her even better shots.

She almost wanted to start there. Crinkling up her face,

she said, "We could start in the fitness room if you want."

He glanced at her sideways. "Don't you want to go for a walk first?"

"Sure," she said, "And afterwards, we can go to the gym."

He shook his head. "You're the only female I know who is happy to watch a guy work out."

"Maybe I'll do some yoga myself this time." She rolled her shoulders several times. "Last night left a little too much tension in the muscles."

"Sorry."

She shrugged. "All's well…and all that."

A comfortable silence ensued as they walked along.

Then, as if he'd been thinking about the issue for a while and the words were just rushing through him, he said, "Is it? Are you over last night, or did it just make it all worse?"

Surprised at his outburst, she said, "I think it's better. I didn't wake up screaming in the night like I would have if this had happened a few years ago. I woke up and was aware that I was safe, understanding it had been a bad dream. It took a while to get back to sleep, but there were other reasons as well."

"Like what?"

"You." She said it honestly, not knowing how else to be. "You've been very patient and understanding with me."

"And?" He motioned to a bench beside a huge flower garden. "Why do I sense a question behind that?"

"It's just I don't want you to feel obligated to do what you're doing."

"Obligated." He rolled the word around on his lips as if testing it, tasting to see what it meant or if there were any hidden meanings behind it. "I don't feel obligated. I'm sorry for what you went through and am happy to help."

She flinched.

"Not the right answer?"

"There is no right or wrong answer. I want to hear the truth."

"But you don't like the answer."

She leaned back on the bench. This big man, this mountain of a man, was twice her size with so much more strength than she could imagine herself having. Look at the way he'd lifted her up to his face last night. He hadn't even struggled, holding her there like a child.

And now, he was worried about having said the wrong thing. "You're a special man, you know."

He lifted an eyebrow. "What brought that on?"

She grinned. "You, trying to help but afraid of saying the wrong thing. I'm glad you are helping me. At the same time, I'd hate to think that this is all about the assignment."

He lifted his shoulders then dropped them. "What does any of this have to do with the assignment?"

And damn if she didn't believe his bewilderment was for real. "Nothing apparently." She laughed, the sound rolling freely across the garden. "I'm just letting doubts color my thinking."

"Look. I'm a real plain, basic man. I'm happy to help you deal with your stuff while we're here. After all, that's why we're here. Right?"

Damn. Okay, so it was about the assignment, the course, and her being a screw-up. Still, the dark growing pit in her stomach had hoped he'd wanted more. She understood he'd given her – and with any luck would continue to give her – a gift. If she left this place a few steps closer to being whole to pick up a relationship with another man – one who might care for her – then it was a huge gift. He'd already done so much, she couldn't put her emotional crap around his neck, too. She wanted him like she'd never wanted another man. She understood men could want a lot of women for a lot of reasons, and few of them were the emotional ones that she needed, but maybe that was okay, too.

It was up to her to keep the dreams in check and work on fixing her reality.

Dreams were fine and all, but the reality was…he wasn't in love with her.

And she damned well better remember that.

KANE FIGURED HE'D done or said something wrong as Tania was quiet all the way back to the hotel. He didn't know what he'd done; he just knew he'd done something. It had been the same with his wife. She would never explain and always left him feeling like he was in the doghouse.

In Tania's case, he wasn't sure what had happened, but it was like she'd flicked a switch. She had gone from being bubbly and happy to being more reserved, as if she was putting him at arm's length, pushing him away.

To hell with that.

He left her to change while he thought about a game plan to get her back to normal, and maybe back into his arms.

He slowed in the act of stripping off his t-shirt. Was that what he wanted? Hell yes. He wanted her in his arms, in his bed, in his life.

He sat down in shock. Was he really saying he wanted a relationship with her? Past the constraints of the seminar? Really? What if she never could get around to having a sexual relationship? Was he ready for that?

When it came to relationships, she'd be work.

He flinched. "But so am I."

Was she interested in him only as the man who could initiate her into a fulfilling sex life without intercourse if need be? He groaned. His mind filled with images of ways to introduce her to the pleasures of the body.

He wasn't the only man who could, but he was the man who wanted the job the most.

But how could he convince her they should continue to see each other after this seminar?

Then he realized what he'd said. "Idiot. You told her you were happy to help her out, not that you wanted to be there for her."

She'd have likely taken his response as being friendly and trying to get through the course, not him being interested in her for her sake.

"Smooth, Kane. Really smooth." Not.

And then there was another aspect to consider – was she interested in him as anything but experimental material? He hoped so. He didn't mind being used in this instance. After all, he'd agreed to it, but what if her interests were only self-serving? He couldn't really blame her…but neither would it make for a start of a relationship.

Then there were his own issues. Trust. Anger. Betrayal.

And none of them seemed important. He'd been feeding the pain to keep it alive to stop him from considering other relationships. Now that he'd found something more important, he could let the hurts ease down where they belonged – in the past.

Damn, he hated when Jenna was right.

CHAPTER 20

TANIA GAVE HERSELF a mental talking-to. The man was gorgeous but disinterested. She needed to take what he offered and let him off the hook. Let him return to his life as he wanted it. The attraction between them was probably just proximity and promise. That there was a man who didn't mind kissing her made her hormones go crazy. Just the promise of dealing with her problems, of finding a man capable of handling her problems, made her jump on board. It wasn't real. Her feelings needed to be acknowledged but not acted upon.

And didn't that sound like something she'd heard in a therapy session.

Damn Jenna and her shrink babble anyway.

At the fitness room, she decided to do some stretches herself. She had her camera and bag to continue working on their project, but at the same time she knew her body needed some work, too. She'd taken the week off and that wasn't good. Her daily routine always included twenty minutes of yoga, and she missed it.

Knowing Kane would get there when he was damn good and ready, she set about moving through her positions.

The door opened when she'd slipped into the third one. In the mirror, she could see Kane open his bag and chalk up his hands, and then he went to work. She tried to focus on her movements, but it was damn hard. The man's body was a powerhouse and a joy to watch. Add in her artistic eye and her fingers were itching to grab her camera.

Another ten minutes and she gave up. Hopping to her feet, she opened her bag and grabbed her camera. It took a moment to set up, then she turned and walked over to Kane. He had a distant, unfocused look on his face as he recovered from a set of sit-ups. Personally, she hated sit-ups, push-ups, and chin-ups. But then again, she wasn't into anything that made her sweat like she'd been in a sauna or made her hurt so bad she wanted to cry.

Kane, on the other hand, seemed to thrive on it.

She shook her head and shifted into her art.

When he switched up to arm curls, she shifted much closer to work. She began taking photos of the muscles as they tightened and released, the film of moisture that rose to the surface, the fine hairs that shifted and moved then became locked in the sweat.

"What can you possibly find interesting in all of this?" Kane asked, his voice laced with irritation.

She took a step back, studied his face, and saw the pain, the frustration, and the anger. It wasn't a good day for him, at least here in the gym. "Do you want me to stop?

He snorted. "I want to go home. This week has been a fucking waste of time."

Ouch. She didn't think he meant her specifically, but as he was here for his own problems, if he wasn't making progress, then he would be pissed. She would be, too, in his shoes. That she was making progress and he was angry spoke volumes about where they both were at this time. It saddened her. "I'm sorry. The seminar is almost over. You should be working on your issues and not helping me with mine."

He spun around from reaching for more weights. "I shouldn't even be here." He waved a hand around. "This isn't my thing. I hate being inactive. I like purpose in my life, action. Not..." he threw up his hands in frustration. "Not whatever this is."

"I understand." And she did, but it didn't help him any.

She took a deep breath and prepared to be blasted. "If there is something I can do to help you deal with your issues, then tell me. I'd be happy to give back."

He stiffened, then relaxed. "Tinkerbelle, you've already helped. But some things just have to work themselves out over time."

"True. But there are some things you just have to jump into and let go. I often wonder if time isn't a crutch more than anything. I look back on the years where I felt I couldn't do anything, wouldn't push my boundaries – and then I never progressed."

"In your case, you couldn't. Some things do take time. In my case..." and he stopped, an odd look coming over his features.

"In your case?"

He sat down on the bench and shook his head. "It's stupid."

"It's not stupid if it matters."

"That's the thing. You said earlier that we feed something to keep it alive. And in my case, that's exactly what happened. I've been feeding something to keep it alive, but it's dead. She's dead. Gone," he said starkly.

"Oh my. Did you lose your wife?"

She raced over to his side, her palm coming to rest on his cheek.

He shook his head, but his gaze was haggard. "No," he said hoarsely. "She aborted my baby and didn't tell me until afterwards. She told me she killed my daughter because she wasn't ready to be a mother."

His tortured gaze rose to lock onto hers. "I've been so angry, but it was more because I was grieving. How could I be so lost, so devastated by the loss of a child not yet born? She killed her. Wouldn't even give her a chance at life."

Tania didn't know what to say. Such a horrible event, and for his wife to have made such a decision without him said a lot about the state of his marriage. A state he himself wouldn't have understood until it was too late.

Compassion welled up inside and she couldn't help herself; she wrapped her arms around him and held him close.

He stiffened, then let himself be held. His arms went around her, holding on to her as the revelations just kept coming. He said, his voice barely above a croak, "It's me I'm really mad at, for not seeing what she'd do. For not having taken better care to avoid a pregnancy in the first place. For making sure my daughter was safe." He parted his knees and pulled her down to his lap. "All this time, I hated her, but deep inside, I hated myself. All this time I told myself that women weren't to be trusted, and it was me I didn't trust."

"I'm sorry," she whispered. "I'm sorry for all three of you."

He stared down at her. "That's the truth, isn't it? There were three injured souls here."

"Yes, but she could have handled it very differently, and she didn't want to. For whatever reason, she wanted to hurt you."

He stared out, a distant look in his eyes. "She was so angry when she found out. Children were in her plans, but down the road, a long ways down the road when she was ready, when the timing was right. She was a big planner, and this blew her plans off course."

"The time is rarely right for a major life event," Tania said, remembering her own pain and shock from so many years ago. Her parents had divorced as a result of it, her mother's life irrevocably changed by her daughter's assault. "It doesn't matter. We have to deal with the hand Mother Nature deals us. It's the *how* that makes us *who* we are."

Kane stared down at her, surprise lighting the chocolate depths.

"When did you get so wise?"

"After years of therapy," she said in a dry tone and smiled. "It's a funny thing, but when you least expect it, a breakthrough does happen and you wonder at your past...a past of just a few moments earlier before you had the epiphany."

His lips kicked up into a smile. "How true."

He leaned back and took a deep breath. "I feel both good and...exhausted."

She patted his shoulder. "I know what you mean."

A glint slipped into his eyes. "Nap time?"

She stared into his deep gaze and then understood. Heat rolled through her, coloring her cheeks. She gasped then giggled. "Oh, Lord." Then she nodded. "Definitely nap time."

His grin turned lethal. He leaned forward, dropped a kiss on her cheek, and whispered in a deep voice, "Your room or mine?"

Instantly, she said in a voice gone hoarse, "Mine."

HOW HAD THEY gone from being distant and irritated to racing like school kids down the hallway? He hoped they didn't meet anyone; Tania needed this.

Hell, he did, too.

His emotions were too raw at the moment to be examined with any intensity, but there was just such a sense of relief sliding off his shoulders with every step he moved further away from the pain. It would never dim his loss but it would firmly be in the past, where it belonged.

If she could get to this same point…wow.

She'd come so far already. Now could she go all the way? He almost groaned as his groin tightened. He hated to think how far away they were from where he wanted to be.

They reached her room undisturbed, and she unlocked the door and they slipped inside. Laughing and giggling like kids, she locked the door and turned to face him.

He opened his arms and she ran into them. God, he loved that.

Damn if he wasn't falling in love with her.

CHAPTER 21

TANIA WOULD DO anything to feel what Kane had made her feel last time. Knowing they had hours ahead of them made her whimper in the back of her throat. Instinct told her to crawl up his frame and go after more.

Pulling back slightly, she gave him a light push toward the bed. "Lie down."

He flipped his shirt over his head and kicked off his shoes. Standing at the end of the bed, arms wide, he fell backwards.

"I'm all yours."

She froze. "Oh, I hope you're right."

He lifted an eyebrow. "I mean it. Be gentle with me, sweetheart."

She grinned and pounced. She grabbed his closest foot and ripped off his sock. He laughed as her hands tickled his feet. He tried to tug his foot away, but she hung on. Releasing the bare one, she fought to get the sock off his other foot.

When he could, he gasped out, "What is this, a sock-free zone?"

She smirked. "Absolutely."

"Good, then you'd better be sockless, too," he warned. "Or else I get to remove them."

"Ha." She quickly stripped off her own socks. "Now I am."

"Good, now how about the pants and shirt, too?"

"Yeah, I don't think so." She shook her head. "I'm not playing that game. You still have your shorts on."

And before she'd figured out what he was doing, Kane lay stretched out before her only wearing white knit boxers. She swallowed hard. He rested his head on his hands and grinned up at her. "Now what are you going to do?"

"Admire you," she said honestly. "You're truly gorgeous."

His gaze widened. As she glanced up to his face, she was startled to see a wash of red working up his neck. "Really? You're okay to lie here in front of me in only your underwear, completely unconcerned, but I give you a compliment and you're embarrassed?"

A sheepish grin washed over his face. "I'll say thank you, and we'll move on."

"On to what?"

"Whatever you want; whatever you're comfortable with trying."

She sighed happily and went to crawl on the bed beside him but stopped. She looked down at her capris. She really wanted some freedom to move. Her t-shirt was more camisole than shirt, but her pants were heavy cotton without any stretch. Taking a deep breath and moving fast, she stripped off her capris, laid them on the empty chair, and turned back to face Kane.

He watched her, a smile on his face. "Doing good, Tinkerbelle."

She grinned; she was doing good. As long as he understood that progress could stop at any time…

Awkwardly, she climbed onto the bed and stared down at his massive body. "You're so big," she whispered.

"Yeah, so are my dad and my brother."

"Really?" At his nod, she turned her attention back to his feet. In a whimsical move, she slipped one leg down to line alongside his foot. His had to have been twice the length of hers and was at least twice as wide.

A laugh rumbled through him. "I guess calling you Tinkerbelle wasn't far off. You are seriously tiny."

She gave an indelicate snort. "I'd never had it pointed out in quite the same way before. I'd have considered myself on the small side, but not like this." She placed a hand on his thigh, feeling it tighten into granite under her gentle touch. "You're so different from me. Your skin is thick, rough; your muscles – powerhouses."

"We're meant to be that way."

She nodded thoughtfully, loving the way his thigh twitched under her fingers, almost playing a rhythm. She stroked down over his kneecap, marveling at the sheer width of the joint. Hers would fit completely inside his with room to spare. "It's hard to believe the massive build."

"It's required to hold this massive body up," he said, amused. "Your kneecaps would crumple under my weight."

She couldn't argue with his logic, her hands now both stroking, learning, and feeling the differences between them. Loving the differences between them. And even more – loving the freedom between them. She sighed. "I know it embarrasses you, but I have to tell you that the artist in me finds you to be a perfect model."

"Model for what?"

"Everything." She lowered her head and dropped a kiss on his thigh. The smooth muscle twitched, so she did it again and again. She laid her cheek down on his thigh, looked down the long expanse of leg, and realized his toes were wiggling. She grinned, shifting so she could see his face. He lay with his eyes closed, accepting, allowing…

"You're a gift, you know."

Startled, he popped his eyes open, "What?" He shook his head. "Hell no, I'm just a normal man."

"One who's willing to lie here like this? That makes you special."

She slid her hand up to the edge of his boxers and stroked along the elastic edge. He bit back a gasp and she smiled. Exploring further, she let her finger slide toward the bulge in the center and watched in awe as it grew beside her fingers. She glanced up at Kane to find him watching her carefully. Then she closed her hand around him. He groaned and arched his head back.

She released him. "I'm so sorry. I didn't mean to hurt you."

He gave a garbled laugh, grabbed her hand, and placed it back on his shaft, wrapping her fingers around him again. "You didn't hurt me."

She moved her fingers experimentally. "Are you sure?"

"I'm sure. It feels wonderful."

"You don't look like you're enjoying this."

This time, he managed a full laugh. "Really, so how does this feel?" He slid his hand over her thigh to caress her bottom, his long fingers cupping her cheek before searching for and locating the silky thong strap between her thighs.

She froze at the first touch of his fingers and moaned softly at the exquisite sensation of his rough finger over her delicate skin. She moved her hips, pushing her cheeks against his hand.

"See, it feels good, but an almost-painful good."

"Yes," she whispered. Emboldened, she squeezed gently,

loving the strangled sound escaping from his lips. "Like that?"

"Just like that. And like this." Once again, he covered her hand and moved it up and down the length of him.

She'd heard of hand jobs, had seen movies of women between the men's legs giving blow jobs. She understood the mechanics but hadn't understood the lure. Now, for the first time, she understood.

She slowly withdrew her hand, loving the way he lifted his hips to follow her. She dropped a kiss at the top elastic band. "I think you're wearing too many clothes."

"Then take them off, baby."

The way he said 'baby' brought up shivers of desire and had her reaching out, snagging the material and pulling it down over his hips. Her gaze caught on the thick organ lying nestled in dark curls. Then, as if knowing it was being observed, it rose up and waved.

She swallowed hard, her mind consumed with the evidence of something she hadn't considered until now. As she removed his boxers and threw them onto the floor, she realized she had to put a stop to this. She stood beside him, now lying nude on the bed, with full expectations of something good to come out of this, but...

"Kane, I hate to tell you this."

She stopped, and he rolled his head toward her. "What's the matter, Tania?"

She motioned to the huge erection that both fascinated and now alarmed her and said, "You aren't going to fit."

KANE GRINNED THEN laughed and finally, unable to contain his amusement, he howled. He snagged her arm and tugged her on top of him, then held her head firmly while looking deep into her eyes. He said, "Do you trust me?"

Immediately, she nodded.

"Right. So trust me a little further. I will fit."

She shot a dubious look at the lower end of the bed, but she was now lying on top of him and couldn't see his anatomy. Good thing. He'd been unable to get the image of being buried deep inside her tiny body since this started. He should have considered that this stage would cause some cold feet but would have bet that fear, not doubt that this would mechanically work, would have been what set her off.

This one he could work with.

He rolled over so they lay side by side and looked into her eyes. Seeing the cloudiness in their dark depths, he said, "Please."

After a long moment, she whispered, "I'm willing to try but you have to understand… I might not make it."

He nodded. He knew that already. He could be in for the most frustrating time of his life, but he'd survive it. If she was willing to give him a chance, he could do no less.

In a slow, easy motion, he rolled her over onto her back. "Good. I think that considering I'm completely nude, you should be, too.

Her gaze widened as her shirt was flipped over her head and…and holy crap. She didn't have a bra on, and the most perfect pair of small, round breasts lay before him. He feasted his eyes on her. "Tinkerbelle, you are gorgeous."

Pink tinged her cheeks.

"Thank you," she whispered. He studied the nervousness in her eyes. "It will be fine, Tania. I promise."

She relaxed slightly. "I hope so."

He lay down beside her and tugged her into his arms

before he kissed her.

Her lips opened immediately, and she wrapped her arms tightly around him. He knew what it took for her to take this step. He was humbled by her trust and was determined to make it good for her.

He kissed her senseless, exploring her lips, feasting on her mouth, smoothing tantalizing kisses across her cheeks and chin before coming back to drown in her nectar again and again. His hand stroked across her belly and traced the line of her ribs before finally cupping her breasts.

She arched beneath him, crying out.

"Shh, it's okay." But she twisted beside him, her body ready even if her mind wasn't. He lowered his head and tugged first one nipple then the other into his mouth. Such beautiful breasts deserved his attention, and he wanted to savor the opportunity.

Tania shivered and twisted. She had no idea what was happening to her. When he slipped his fingers through the patch of curls, she cried out and squeezed her thighs shut. He coaxed her thighs apart and slid his fingers into the dampness.

"Oh God, Kane."

"I know. Take it easy, sweetheart. It's supposed to be like this."

She flipped her head from side to side. "How can this be good? The tension…I feel wound-up, tied up in knots."

He slipped one finger inside, and her hips arched as she cried out again. He worked a second finger inside, cursing at his own urgency. She was so damn tight. He dropped his forehead on her flat belly and took several deep breaths. He could do this.

He pulled his fingers out, then thrust them in and back

out. Sliding lower down, he pulled her thighs wide enough apart to make a place for himself, and he tasted her.

She shrieked. Her hands burrowed into his hair. "Oh, God, what are you doing?"

He smiled and replaced his fingers with his tongue.

She exploded seconds later, crying out as she rained all over him. He lifted himself up, fitted himself to the heart of her, and slowly entered.

She twisted and turned, pinned in place by an indomitable force. He searched her features but there was no fear, no panic. But something had unsettled her.

Inexorably, he slid deeper and deeper.

"I can't. No more. You don't fit."

Then she said the words that broke his heart. "Please, stop."

He shuddered in place, denial screaming through him. He was desperate to plunge in and finish this, her cries be damned, but he knew he couldn't do it.

Sweat beads popped out on his forehead, and he lowered his head until it rested on hers.

Then he closed his eyes. His body gave another long shudder as he regained another measure of control.

She whimpered. "I'm sorry."

"Shhh. Don't be." He didn't want her to be sorry. She'd taken such a huge step already; saying the wrong thing now could set her way back.

"I am, though." She opened her tear-filled eyes, and he felt her 'sorry' like an arrow to his heart. She figured it was her. There was such defeat in her gaze. Shame. "I can't do this. I won't ever be able to do this."

She started to weep. If there was ever anything guaranteed to kill his ardor, it was that. But he'd be damned if he'd let this be the ending. She *could* do this, but she had to know she could, and in order for that to happen, she had to trust him.

"Tania, easy, sweetie."

She sniffled.

He shifted to the side, sliding his hands down to her hips, and snuggled her tightly against him. He'd be dammed if he withdrew completely.

"Is this better?" he murmured, dropping kisses on her cheek, her nose, and finally on her mouth.

She nodded, shifting her hips experimentally. "I'm sorry," she said again.

He smiled. "Don't be. Look at how far you've come."

She frowned, shifted again, and looked down at their fused bodies. "Are you still inside?"

"I am." *Just not very far, unfortunately.*

"But..." and her frown deepened as she tried to think it through. She wiggled a little more, and then grinned. "I can feel you in there."

"I should hope so," he said with feeling.

"So, you do fit?" she asked cautiously a moment later.

He laughed. "I said I would. It's just so new to you. And yes, I'm big and you're little, but we fit together just fine."

"Only you're not as big as you were before, right?"

And damn if she didn't tighten her inner muscles. His response was immediate. Her eyes widened and she shifted again, then again. He rolled over so she was lying on his chest and gently nudged her up.

She sat up and gasped.

He shuddered.

"Oh my." She shifted from side to side then tilted her hips forward and back. Her inexperienced exploration was going to kill him.

"That's…different."

"Ya think?" his voice came out gritty and deep. A ripple slipped down his body.

"Oh, you like that, don't you?" She leaned forward, her hips lifting.

He groaned and grabbed her hips to stop her from lifting off completely. As she sat down again, he groaned, and she smiled, a sweetly enchanting female smile.

He knew he was in trouble. She lifted and lowered herself again and then repeated the motion. Each time, her movement settled her slightly lower and he went slightly deeper. *Oh, dear God.*

A deep sigh slid from his chest. "Yesss," he whispered. "Sooo good."

He opened his eyes to see her face tilted to the ceiling, head back, long hair drifting down her back. But it was the look of inner concentration on her face that caught and held his attention. She was beautiful at any time, but like this, riding after something she didn't understand but knowing she was on the right path, she rode faster and faster and…stopped as her body exploded. She cried out and came to a shuddering stop.

"No." He gripped her hips and drove upwards, once, twice, and a groan ripped out of his throat as he climaxed.

She collapsed down on top of him and closed her eyes.

"I did it," she whispered. "Finally."

And fell silent.

CHAPTER 22

TANIA WOKE UP hours later, alone.

She shifted to study the room and almost cried out at the unexpected achiness. How come she had to pay after something that felt so good? And froze.

Oh, dear God. They hadn't used birth control. With everything else going on, her mind had been worrying about so much already that she hadn't once considered the issue. She fell back, scared.

Her instinctive reaction was shock. Her mind was saying this was not the right time, and she flinched. Hadn't Kane's wife said something similar? No, they weren't in the same situation. She'd been married, in an obviously steady sexual relationship, and should have had some method of birth control that worked for them. And Kane had likely thought she'd had some protection, but he'd never asked…and God help her, she'd never even considered the issue once.

As she laid there, her fingers splayed over her belly, it was hard to be upset. She'd wanted children since forever. If it turned out she was pregnant, she couldn't do anything but see this as a gift. It was not how she had planned it, and it was not how she would have chosen for it to happen, but thinking of a tiny child growing inside her right now made her toes curl with joy.

What would Kane think?

After his wife's actions, she knew how he'd feel about it. He would take responsibility and be willing to step up, but that's not what she wanted. She didn't want a child between them to be a responsibility. She wanted such a thing to be a joy. Beautiful. Special. Wanted. Yet she knew she'd love this miracle child, if she was so lucky, enough for both of them.

Then reality returned. Her cycle was due to start in just a couple of days, so chances were good she wasn't pregnant. It had happened to other people – but she wasn't that lucky.

It would be better at this point if she weren't pregnant. *Liar.* She'd be delighted if it turned out she was. Still, there couldn't be any more of this without responsible birth control. She had no idea which way to go, or even if there would be another incident. The seminar would be over tomorrow. They had all day to work on the projects before presenting them to Jenna just before noon. The afternoon would be a summary of the course, and she and Kane would be the last to present their homework. Thank God. She hadn't finished or made it anywhere close to finishing the project.

She scrambled out of bed and grabbed her laptop. It was after dinner. In fact, it was almost bedtime. She opened her laptop to find a note tucked inside from Kane.

Instantly, she gave a happy sigh. He hadn't left without a goodbye.

"Hey sleepyhead. I'm going to get dinner and will bring back something for you. If you want to call me, here's my number. Otherwise, I'll be back soon."

Her heart melted. Not only had he not been gone long, but he'd thought of her enough to bring her something to eat.

Then they had to do their homework.

She turned on her laptop, grabbed her camera, and started downloading pictures.

There were hundreds. While waiting, she stepped into the shower but kept her hair up and out of the water. She didn't want to sleep with it wet, and if Kane was coming back, she really didn't want wet hair to dampen his ardor.

In the water, she slowly moved the sponge across her body, wondering why everything felt so different, alive. As if his touch, their lovemaking, had awakened millions of nerve endings she'd never known about.

Considering the physical differences, she had to stop and consider – how did she feel mentally? Emotionally? Spiritually?

Standing under the heavy force while hot water beat down on her skin, she smiled, letting the water wash over her. She felt…wonderful. Renewed. Her heart was exploding with happiness, joy, love, and yes… relief. She'd made love with Kane. Sure, she'd had a little freak out, but with his help, she'd pushed through to a surprise ending. She'd never thought it could be that good. Sure, she'd heard other girls giggling over their sexual encounters and sharing stories – something she couldn't ever imagine doing about Kane. He was too special, the stories too intimate, the emotions too overwhelming. No matter where she and Kane went as a couple, she'd always be grateful for what he'd done.

He didn't want her gratitude. She knew that instinctively, but he had it regardless – forever.

She didn't know when the first tears started. Once started, though, she couldn't hold back and they cascaded down her cheeks to blend with the hot water beating down on her face. Then she started to sob. She wrapped her arms around her chest and cried.

She couldn't even begin to voice the outpouring of emotion. But as if a huge scab had been ripped off – a premature scab, as if the wound underneath hadn't reached that point of healing – the pus buried deep inside poured out.

The hot water beat down on her body as she cried for the little girl she'd been back then, for the lost years of innocence and for the many years in between when she'd existed in only half a world. The years after where she'd tried hard to be normal but had been faking it all the way.

She hadn't known how badly damaged she'd been until now, how thin and fragile her psyche. Now, her deepest fears had been opened and the darkest poisons festering inside released.

Time passed. She didn't know how long she'd stood under the water. She hadn't been aware that she'd dropped to a crouch, rocking herself back and forth, until strong arms grabbed her.

She shrieked and flailed her arms.

"Easy, Tinkerbelle, it's just me." Kane's voice washed over her, and she collapsed, sobbing against his chest.

"Sorry," she whispered over and over again. The water was turned off, and she was bundled up in a towel and carried out to the bedroom.

"You have nothing to be sorry for." He held her so carefully, as if she'd break. She'd have laughed if she could have, because she was already broken.

Her sobs slowed and finally turned into a damp sniffling by the time he had her tucked in the bed, a second towel moving briskly over her hair.

When he finished, he picked up the hairbrush and brushed her hair in long, sure strokes. She tilted her head back and let him.

It felt so good. It brought up one more piece of poison to be examined and maybe, if she was lucky, released.

In a hoarse whisper, she said, "He broke my ribs, my collarbone, and a finger. He was so angry."

The brushing stopped. For a long moment, she thought he was going to leave, but then the gentle movement resumed. Barely leashed anger resounded in his voice as he said, "Why was he angry?"

"He wanted a child, like seven or eight. Instead, I was thirteen and already going through puberty."

KANE WANTED TO kill someone, a specific someone. He wanted to pulverize the asshole that had taken a beautiful child and broken her because he'd made assumptions based on her size. That the asshole was a child predator to begin with made him sick of his sex.

That Tania had been dealing with this for so long, without a break, without an end, said so much about the person she was inside.

"Is that why you were crying in the shower?"

She immediately shook her head. "I'm not sure what started the tears. But it's like an old injury was finally brought to light so I could release it. Sort of like a purging. I'm so tired." She yawned. "I feel empty. But at the same time, I feel renewed, as if now I can fill those empty places with something good."

She curled up on the bed and fell asleep – just like that.

Kane stared down at her, wondering again at the trust in him. She'd gone from shocked and lashing out at him in panic before she understood who was in the shower with her to instant acceptance, letting him look after her.

Now she slept with the innocence of a child.

But her admission, something she'd never told anyone – yeah, her admission had ripped his heart out. So much pain and horrible memories being brought to the light of day and then released.

It was exhausting work. She needed to rest. He looked down at his soaking-wet clothing, the hairbrush in his hand. "What am I going to do?" Her dinner was sitting on the desk. He'd passed Jenna in the hallway and had given Tania's excuses for missing dinner. Jenna hadn't missed much in that sharp glance of hers, but after making sure Tania was indeed fine, she'd walked away. There would be a therapy session tomorrow. A good thing for Tania. She needed someone experienced to help her at this stage.

Did she still need him?

And what did he need?

Right now, he could use a conversation with Jenna. He pulled out his cell phone and called her. "Do you have time for coffee?" he asked, thankful she was here at the hotel and basically on-call for the attendees. Stuff came up and people needed to talk. It was the first time he'd done this, though.

"Yes," she said instantly. "Shall we go to the coffee shop, or do you want to meet elsewhere?"

"Coffee shop in five minutes." He closed the cell phone, grabbed his hotel key card, and left. With any luck, Tania would sleep until he got back.

Jenna was waiting for him.

He slid into the bench opposite her, ordered coffee, and waited silently for it to be delivered.

"I need help." There, cool and direct – his style. "For Tania."

Her gaze narrowed and her lips twitched. "In what way?"

"She's had a major breakthrough, like a traumatic type of breakthrough. I don't know what to do for her."

"Tell me."

He took a deep breath, then something in him made him stop. He winced. "She might not like me talking to you. It's personal."

"Then let me tell you, and you can nod or shake your head." Damned if Jenna didn't run through the list of their lovemaking, bonding, bringing up old memories, nightmares, and an outpouring sob-fest.

He nodded, nodded, and just kept nodding. "Damn, you do know."

She smiled gently, so much compassion and understanding in her gaze that he realized she knew so much because she'd lived it herself. Then another piece of the puzzle called 'Jenna' slipped into place. She helped others because she came from a place of having healed herself.

Feeling better, he said, "So, what do I do?"

"Be there for her." Jenna's response was instant and confident, but then she ruined it. "If you can."

And that allowed doubt to enter his mind. "I don't know," he said in a low voice. "This is deep stuff."

"And now it's not so deep. All hurts, once opened to the light of day, have the power to heal. When we keep them buried and hidden, they only fester."

"She's come a long way."

"She has." Jenna sipped her coffee calmly, waiting.

He sighed. "I don't know if I'm up for this."

She nodded. "Then you need to say goodbye to her, knowing that your part in her healing journey is over."

Her quick response saying he could leave pissed him off. "I didn't say I wanted to get *out* of this, I'm just not sure I can *do* this."

"Understood." She waited.

Damn, he hated that. He stared moodily out the window, the late sun sinking in the horizon, throwing gorgeous hues on the hills surrounding them. The campus was beautiful but like everything, there was a dark side to it.

"I want to know her whole story, but at the same time, the bits and pieces I do know make me so angry."

She sipped her coffee. He turned to look at her to see that she was studying his hand. He stared down at his big mitt and understood he wasn't clenching his fist, even though he was angry. At a level he hadn't seen in a long time, it wasn't physical anger. He was hurting. For her. He knew he could never right the wrong. He could only help her make the most of every day, but it was a big job. Maybe too big. "I don't think I can help her."

"You already have."

"So much more needs to be done."

"That's for her to do."

"And what do I do for her?" he cried. "It seems so little."

"What you are doing is so very much."

He stopped and stared at her. "How? What am I doing?"

"You're caring for her, standing by her, being there for her, supporting her as she walks this difficult journey. That's something she's never had."

Jenna smiled, a warm loving movement that fascinated him. "You are doing the best thing anyone can do for her – you are loving her."

That was when he recognized what his next step needed to be.

To go back and keep loving her; not to let her put distance between them, to throw up barriers, to keep herself inside and him on the outside. But to give them a chance – to see what they could be. He had more insecurities than he'd ever had about a relationship, but the rewards were exponential as well.

He didn't want to miss this chance.

He shook his head. "It's really that simple, isn't it?"

"It usually is, but what about your issues? How are you handling your problems while you've been helping her deal with hers?"

He smiled at the way-too-wise woman sitting across from him. "That's the thing, isn't it? While I was so focused on helping her, I stopped thinking about my own problems and when I turned around, my anger was gone. It had dissipated, no longer letting me hide from the real problem; my wife's betrayal, the guilt of not having been able to save my child, and the grief of losing my daughter."

She reached across the table and laid her hand gently on his. "Sounds like you've been through a lot yourself."

"And came out on the other side without really realizing what I'd done," he admitted. "I was so focused on Tania, I'd let go of my own problems."

"It's called healing. And it often happens when we're more concerned about helping someone else."

He lifted his cup, drained it, and put it down. "Thank you. I'm going back to Tania so she doesn't wake up alone. Maybe tomorrow you can check in and see how she's doing."

"I will," Jenna promised. Knowing she watched him but not caring, Kane stood up and headed back to where he really wanted to be.

At Tania's side.

It was only as he approached her doorway that he realized he didn't have the key card to get back inside her room.

He dropped his forehead on the door. Shit.

CHAPTER 23

TANIA WOKE UP with a sore throat, burning eyes, and a happy heart.

She'd take the nasty physical symptoms any day – as long as she got to keep the happy heart. She had no idea what time it was. All she'd done for the last day was a mix of emotional outburst – sleep – emotional outburst – collapse.

She sat up in bed and looked around. She was alone.

And damn if she wasn't starting to hate that.

Then again, he could only be expected to be there so long. And she needed to give him the freedom to leave. It was the last day of the seminar, and although she didn't give a damn about completing her homework and handing it over to Jenna, she did care about fulfilling her own commitment to her healing. Without her assignment, she'd never have gotten here – she might have in another way at another time, but the fact was, she was here.

And she was so grateful. Checking her laptop for the time, she found out it was six in the morning. She needed to get the homework done.

She needed to free Kane. Make him understand that she was grateful he'd been here, but if this wasn't where he wanted to be…then that was okay, too.

It wasn't, but she wasn't going to try to keep him on a hook. She'd gotten over worse, and coming into this seminar, she'd have been jumping for joy to think of making it this far.

Determined to end the seminar in a good frame of mind, she set about sorting the latest images. As she worked, the theme started to build more in her mind. She planned on printing the images on the hotel printer. She needed the images in black and white, but they had to tell the story properly.

She worked for a solid hour and felt like she was making progress as she found an image of Kane, relaxed, happy, and almost carefree. She'd taken it when they'd gone for a walk yesterday. He'd been giddy, almost running back to the hotel room. Excited. Natural.

A little later, she realized she was hungry and spied the restaurant bag on the desk. She hopped up to see what Kane had brought her last night. A couple sandwiches were nestled inside a takeout carton. Perfect. She made herself a cup of coffee and polished them both off. Apparently, lovemaking and healing had improved her appetite. She could just imagine the others' comments. At seven, she called down to the front desk and asked about printing the images, then she emailed them to the receptionist, who promised to print them and hole punch them for her.

Tania dressed and packed up her room. Since it was the end of the seminar, she'd elected to leave as soon it was over. She didn't know if other participants were staying another night, but she needed to get back to her normal world.

She'd be sorry to leave. It would hurt in a way. This place would always stay in her memories. A special place, a special time, and a special man.

Once she was ready to go, she decided to check out and leave her bags at the reception area. She could collect them at the end of the morning session. She needed to sort the printed pictures and put a few comments on a couple of them.

With a last look around, she stopped, grabbed her camera, and took several pictures to remember this room by before she took her leave.

Downstairs, she handed over her keys and luggage and accepted the pictures in return. Now, if she could find a way to tie the pages together – a small strip of leather would be perfect – but such a thing was highly unlikely.

"Do you need anything else?"

"Now that you mention it," she said, "Any chance you have a strip of leather of any kind hanging around?"

The woman's gaze widened. "I have a single shoelace that's been sitting in this drawer since forever, would that work?"

She opened her drawer and pulled out one long, single strand.

"Perfect." Borrowing scissors, Tania cut the strip into three equal pieces. Then with her pages and strips, she moved to a comfy seating arrangement in the lobby and went to work. First, she used the laces to tie the pages together in the three different punched holes. Then with the black marker, she wrote *"Skin"* on the title page. Then she added a couple more lines.

Next, she turned to the first image. On that page, she wrote *"The beginning…"*

After that, using the minimum number of words possible, she explained the steps that Kane had gone through to push himself to do what he needed to do to get the job done. Even though he hadn't seen the journey for what it was at the time, it had ended up being his journey and, through that, her journey. As one had healed, it had triggered healing in the other. They'd been perfect partners. On another page, she had a picture of Kane's hand held out toward her. She titled it *"The Gift – Acceptance."*

On the next page, she had an image of her hand she'd taken in her hotel room, outstretched as if to meet his hand. She titled that page *"Acceptance of the gift – another gift of acceptance."*

On the last page, she had a picture – the only one she really disliked as far as clarity went – but it was powerful in its message. The picture was of her hand being held in Kane's hand. Hers tiny and his huge, but hers cradled very gently by this powerful man.

She titled this last image *"A gift offered and a gift returned".*

By the time she was done, she had to sniffle back tears. She flicked thorough the images again and felt like the theme *was* the title. In none of the images was there at any time a piece of clothing, not even a little bit of material to denote clothing existed. In fact, the images stripped Kane down to the basic man inside and out. No artifice. No hiding. No covering up. He was who he was, and it was showed here in all his natural splendor. As natural and as honest as the day he was born, he was wearing the only thing he couldn't remove – his skin.

KANE WOKE UP with a shock of feeling like he was in the wrong place. He bolted upright and threw off his covers. He was in his room. Memories flooded back. He'd taken the wrong hotel key when he went to meet Jenna.

Tania would have woken up alone.

And he'd lost the opportunity to wake her up gently, slowly, lovingly.

Now he realized it was morning, and although he hoped she might still be asleep, she could also have already headed down to the restaurant for breakfast. He dressed, packed, and leaving his stuff behind for the moment, raced down to her room. He knocked, but there was no answer. He knocked again. Then kicking himself again for having taken the wrong key last night, he went to check the restaurant. But he couldn't find her. He frowned. Walking over to the reception desk, he asked the receptionist if Tania had been by.

"She's checked out."

He froze. "Pardon?"

The woman gave him a bright smile. "She was up bright and early, handed back her key, and has officially checked out." She glanced behind her. "Oh, but her luggage is still here. She's part of the seminar, right? So she's likely headed in that direction."

Thanking her, Kane took off to search for Tania. If her luggage was still here, then she was, too. That was all that mattered. He'd find her somehow. Ten minutes later, he spotted Jenna exiting the elevator. "Jenna, have you seen Tania?" He quickly explained about her checking out but still being here and his not being able to find her.

"There are lots of little seating arrangements throughout the hotel. She could be in any one of those. She also might have gone for a walk."

He nodded and turned to look out the front door. She might be out there. He glanced at his watch. "We're starting in what, a half hour?"

"Less. I'm grabbing some tea and going over there now.

We're starting early so I can get into the presentations."

He winced. "Right. The homework."

She laughed lightly. "I presume that's what she's doing right now."

"Oh, most likely." And he'd forgotten all about it. "I'll catch up with you in class."

He did a quick search of the hotel. Not finding Tania, he decided he needed some coffee. He'd rather have something much stronger…

With cups of coffee in both hands, he headed to start the last day of the seminar. He couldn't even begin to explain to his brother what he'd gone through here. Trying to explain what he'd learned from the seminar would be tough because what he'd learned had come from Tania herself, and that wouldn't have happened except for that damn homework. Damned if Jenna hadn't planned that all along.

How could she have known? Had she known? No, surely not. She didn't have any psychic abilities that would allow her to see who would be the best fit with another. But she'd created a magical opportunity when she'd paired Kane with Tania. And he'd asked her to change it.

She'd refused. Thank God.

He walked into class to find Tania sitting beside Robin, both of them involved in an animated conversation. He almost didn't want to interrupt, but Robin spotted him first. She said something to Tania, who spun around. He caught the barest whisper of relief in her eyes, and she smiled up at him.

"Hey. Is one of those for me?"

"Yeah, I wasn't sure how long you'd sleep."

"I woke up early, ate the sandwiches you brought me last night, and then finished the homework."

"Yeah, about that homework." He'd always done his fair share on group projects, but right now he felt like he'd let her down. "I'm sorry I haven't contributed much."

She laughed. "You are so wrong. You contributed the most. Wait until you see it."

"Shouldn't I be adding something to it?" he asked, curious now. He'd seen her theme, and that had made him pause. He'd planned to clarify her thoughts on that subject but had completely forgotten about it with everything else going on. He presumed she hadn't put any images in the project that he'd not be happy about, but as only Jenna and the two of them were going to see it, he could live with it regardless.

"You can if you want to." She handed it over, but Jenna walked in just then and started to wrap up the seminar. She had several guest speakers in to talk with them about the healing journey as she took groups aside and went over their projects.

The morning passed quickly as the speakers were both witty and fun, and although they never made light of their own painful pasts, they showed how far they'd come. After seeing Tania's major growth, Kane had so much more appreciation for them. He'd barely had a chance to flick through the project Tania had put together, but he did read and tried to absorb what she'd done. The depth of what she'd captured astonished him.

The title amused him and confused him until he slowly recognized that there was only skin showing in each of the images. The deepest parts of him had been laid bare by her camera. He was alternately embarrassed and awed by her skill. He understood the captions but thought she might have given him more credit than he was due, but then he came to the last few pages and he stopped. Damn if his eyes weren't trying to burn with tears. He saw his hand outstretched and had no recollection of when she could have taken the image, then turned the page to see her hand unfurling, hesitantly, carefully, but still making the effort.

He turned the page to see the two of them holding hands and realized she hadn't created a homework project, but had instead created a work of art.

Only there was one thing missing.

He leaned over. "Do you still have that marker?"

She pulled it out and handed it over without saying anything. She watched him though, a question in her eyes. He smiled, and on the last page he added three words.

Jenna walked up behind them as he finished.

"Tania and Kane, it's your turn."

CHAPTER 24

TANIA WANTED TO see what Kane had written, but there was no time. Jenna held her hand out for the project and Kane passed it over. She shot Kane a look and whispered, "What did you write?"

He gave her a small smile and said, "You'll have to wait and see."

She rolled her eyes at him. Nervous now that Jenna, with her eyes that saw too much, would read more into the project than Tania had intended, Tania took her seat. The three of them sat at a table where they could all look at the project. In the background, the speaker was going into another story as the group before them took their seats.

Tania wanted to go back to the others and skip this part, but it wasn't to be.

Jenna held it up and read the title. "Skin. What a powerful title." Then she started at the top of the title page and proceeded to read it out loud,

"Skin

A journey of healing

A journey for healers

A journey from the inside out."

"Isn't it, though," Kane said.

Jenna glanced up, her gaze going from one to the other, putting them both in the spotlight of her gaze that saw too much, and said, "Is there anything you want to say about the project before I take a look?"

Kane glanced over at Tania and raised an eyebrow.

Tania shook her head, suddenly tongue-tied and wishing she was anywhere but here.

Jenna smiled. "Then let's take a look."

She turned to the first image where Kane stood staring wistfully, yearning for something in the distance. Tania knew he was staring at a sailboat, but she'd cropped the image so only his face showed. Jenna turned the page, stopping to read the caption and study the images.

Only once while she worked her way through the pages did she say anything. She said, "You are truly gifted with your camera, Tania."

Tania wiggled, a bit uncomfortable with such a personal project being seen for the first time. It said a lot about Kane. She hoped he didn't mind, but it also said a lot about her. She knew that a part of her did mind. The rest of her said deal with it.

It was why she had come, to bring light to her darkest places. She'd done that big time.

After what she'd been through so far at the seminar, this was nothing.

She could do this.

She sighed. "Thank you. It's something I really enjoy doing."

Jenna moved from page to page, stopping to read and study the captions. At one point, she looked up to study the two of them, both so silent and still, and then continued her progress without saying a word. When she finally got to the page where Kane's hand was outstretched, Jenna smiled, and maybe it was Tania's imagination, but she thought Jenna's eyes were over-bright. When she got to Tania's hand tentatively held out, Tania knew she was correct.

Then she turned to the last page and sniffled, then sighed happily. She lifted her teary eyes first to Tania and then to Kane, and her smile warmed. "It's beautiful. Sincerely, heartwarmingly beautiful."

"Tania is responsible for the entire project. She took the pictures, put this collection together, and added the captions." Kane had to say honestly. He couldn't take credit for Tania's success. "I only added one piece to the project."

But Tania was shaking her head. "Not true. You were there every step of the way."

Jenna turned to Kane. "Which part did you add, Kane?"

He grinned sheepishly. "The last line."

Jenna looked down. Turning the last page over, her eyes watered again.

"What does it say?" Tania asked, curiosity getting the better of her. She wished he'd told her first.

Jenna looked from Kane to her. "You haven't read what he wrote down?"

Tania shook her head. She jumped up and ran around so she could see for herself. On the last page, in thick bold printing, Kane had added, "To Be Continued..."

She gasped and burst into tears.

Kane stood up and opened his arms.

She ran into them and sobbed as they closed securely around her.

This was what she'd always wanted. The only thing she could say she'd never had.

A man to love her – broken, mending, or healed; someone who could love her for who she was, regardless of where she'd been or what she'd been through. And she'd finally found him.

Kane.

Author's Note

Thank you for reading Skin! If you enjoyed the book, please take a moment and leave a short review.

Dear reader,

I love to hear from readers, and you can contact me at my website: www.dalemayer.com or at my Facebook author page. To be informed of new releases and special offers, sign up for my newsletter or follow me on BookBub. And if you are interested in joining Dale Mayer's Reader Group, here is the Facebook sign up page.
http://geni.us/DaleMayerFBGroup

Cheers,
Dale Mayer

Scars

Buy this book at your favorite vendor.

Some scars are visible…

Some scars are hidden…

The worst scars are buried deep inside…

Robin and Sean are existing in their private worlds. Hiding in plain sight, not really living, definitely not thriving. They both need to move forward… if they can.

Yet the price of success is pain as they confront issues that have plagued them for years. They're so different, with such opposite problems. Yet they complement each other – or at least they will, if they can work through their issues and find each other.

This is a story of pain and sorrow, joy and success… and… love.

Broken and... Mending

Skin

Scars

Scales (of Justice)

Broken but... Mending 1-3

Previews

Second Chances

Go ahead. Take Charge of your life. Move forward...if you can...

Changing her future means letting go of her past. Karina heads to a weekend seminar and discovers the speaker is the person she needs to move on from. But she soon realizes bigger issues are facing her...

Brian has moved on, at least he'd believed he had... until he sees Karina in his audience...and realizes he's been lying to himself.

Passion pulls them together, love binds them together, but a revengeful enemy determines to keep the two apart...and destroy them both.

Second Chances Sample

Chapter 1

HER HEART RACING, Karina pushed open the glass double doors and walked into the almost deserted pub. Her breath quickened as she searched the faces of the few patrons inside. *Had he left already?* Or was Brian Saunders somewhere here, drowning his sorrows? Wendy, Brian's girlfriend of two years, had broken up with him and taken off for Europe, or some such thing. Karina knew she should feel sorry for him, but instead her mind wouldn't stop pestering her.

Here's your chance. One last shot to make him notice you before you go home and never see him again.

That the timing sucked wouldn't stop her.

Besides, if anyone asked, she was just here having a drink. And she could use one. Her last exam was done. She'd finally finished school and damn if she didn't feel like crying instead of cheering.

"Hey, Karina, thought you'd have booked it by now."

She waved at one of several friends having a good time at a nearby table. Most of the students who'd finished exams had already left, and the few stragglers writing tomorrow were either cramming or here trying to forget about writing in the morning.

"Nah. Leaving in the morning. It's a long drive and I *so* don't want to deal with that tonight. Or the ferry."

That elicited several nods. Anyone who lived on Vancouver Island knew about ferry woes to the mainland. She'd tossed around the idea of staying on the island, had even looked for work, but nothing had come of it, so she was heading home to Vancouver. Victoria, and the university in particular, would stay a happy memory. And, in some ways, a tough one.

She ordered a draft at the bar and turned around to take another look. Maybe she'd missed Brian in her first skim.

Shit. Ian Blackburn was here, too. And he'd seen her. Shit, shit, and triple shit. He'd always been super friendly to her, but there was something about him that gave her the creeps. And then last week she'd seen another side of him altogether. A professor in one of the classes they'd been in together had given Ian a poor grade on an assignment. Ian had lost it…big time. Someone had even called campus security to get him out of the lecture hall. He'd turned into something that terrified her and probably every other student there. She shuddered at the memory.

Karina turned around and glanced the other way, deliberately putting her back to Ian.

And there he was. *Brian.*

Her heart sighed even as it started to pound. She should go over to him. He looked sad, like he'd lost his best friend. Which, after the end of a two-year relationship, she guessed he had. But Karina told herself she was still a friend, right? Albeit a casual one, but still… They'd had classes together, the odd beer-and-pizza night as part of a group. That kind of thing. He had no idea that she'd been in love with him for a long time. She'd been careful to keep her feelings hidden. He

hadn't been free and she wasn't the type to break up relationships.

She checked out the other half of the bar before her gaze
zinged back to Brian. He lifted his beer bottle and poured
the remaining golden liquid down his throat. Slamming the
empty down, he reached for the spare, waiting. Damn, she
hated to see him like this.

All right. She was going to go over there. Just a sip of
beer for courage, first. She raised her glass to her lips.

"Karina. I'm glad you're here. I was hoping to see you
before you left. May I sit?"

Ian. Shit. He'd somehow evaded her awareness and seated himself on the barstool next to her without her knowing.
This was what she got for being nice and polite to a guy who
mistook it for encouragement and, frankly, gave her the
willies.

She attempted a smile behind her glass as she drowned a
big gulp. She had to get away. Now.

"Sorry, I came here to meet someone." She said it lightly, dismissively. She'd planned to wait another minute or two
before approaching Brian, but Ian's crowding was forcing her
hand. "Oh, there he is. Brian."

She got up and waved in Brian's direction, tossing a
good-bye smile at Ian.

His brows came together in a dark vee and his lips
thinned, the expression causing her smile to falter and her
stomach to heave. His thick nose and heavy brows might
indicate a Mediterranean ancestry, but the darkness in his
eyes gave her the spooks.

"I hadn't realized."

Keeping her face averted she took another big step and
cast a glance back, relief washing over her when he didn't

follow, but instead walked back to his seat.

Well, she'd started down this road, so…

"Hey." She slapped a bright, friendly smile on her face and sat down across from Brian. Now that she was safely seated her unease over Ian abated, even while her heart lurched at the deep unhappiness on Brian's face.

He looked up at her, a lopsided attempt at a smile peeking out. "Hi, Karina. I'm not good company right now."

"Oh." She didn't know what to say. His pain was a palpable thing. Impulsively, she reached across the table and laid her hand on his. "I heard and I'm sorry."

Surprise lit the dark depths of his chocolate eyes.

When he didn't say anything, she stood. She'd intruded on his private pain, and that wasn't right. She turned to leave.

"Wait." His husky voice reached out to her. "Please, don't go."

She smiled warmly at him and sat back down.

She stayed there for several more rounds as they talked deep into the night. Once or twice she glanced over at Ian. Every time she looked he appeared to be seething with anger as he stared toward her and Brian. She shuddered.

"This place is closing soon." She tugged Brian to his feet. "Come on, you look ready to drop."

"I'm not that bad," he protested, but allowed himself to be shuffled out the door. The cool night air hit them and snapped some of the buzz away. Karina looked at the stars, her heart full and happy. Not exactly a dream date, but it was Brian…and her…alone.

"Let's go to my place. I think I have a bottle of wine," he suggested.

"You're going to fall asleep before you ever get it open,"

she scoffed as she fell into step beside him.

He looked at her, his little-boy expression pleading that it couldn't possibly be bedtime already. "I don't want to be alone tonight," he admitted softly. "Please come share a bottle of wine with me." There was only a slight slur to his voice and she'd had just enough to drink to feel the same.

Besides, she didn't want the night to end either. It might not be the wisest move but she couldn't come up with any convincing reasons why she shouldn't spend the last few hours with him.

She gave in.

He grinned at her, wrapping an arm around her shoulders. "How come we didn't do this before?" His sloppy grin made her heart laugh. "We should have. I've always liked you."

Magical words.

They walked toward his room, arms around each other, talking, murmuring in low voices. The heat of his voice, the tenor of his words, the glow of moonlight, Brian's touch – it was magic. And she wanted more. She wanted it all. Tonight.

THE COUPLE WALKED down the path, sliding in and out of view. He'd hidden in the trees thinking to see where Brian was taking Karina. And hoping his instinctive guess was wrong.

But no; there she was. Ian thought he'd missed her leaving. But no, she'd left with Brian. Why? *Why Brian?* Brian was nothing. And he had a girlfriend. Or he'd had a girlfriend. According to the gossip, he'd just been dumped.

How could Karina do such a thing? It's not like Brian

was in any shape to enter another relationship right now. Had she no respect. For him? Or for herself?

He stood in the shadows of the trees that darkened the path and watched them make their way to Brian's dorm. Anger simmered inside.

Brian had many girls fawning all over him. He didn't need Karina. He'd only cast her off later.

Karina deserved better. If she weren't so blinded by Brian's flashy looks, she'd realize it. She'd be sorry later.

Damn Brian to hell.

SATISFACTION THRUMMED THROUGH Karina's body as she collapsed beside Brian in the wee hours of the morning. Her skin was damp and her body buzzed from their heated lovemaking. "Who'd have thought?" she whispered into the darkness.

A deep rumble rolled out from his chest as he attempted to speak but couldn't. She grinned. She'd brought him to this. She'd been the one he'd turned to tonight. Not Wendy, but her – Karina. Maybe she shouldn't have jumped at the opportunity…but she'd needed the chance to show him how good they could be together. How perfect.

And given that exams were over and all students going their separate ways, it had been now or never.

It seemed she'd loved him for so long. Always an acquaintance, never quite a friend and always superficial, kept on the outside…the last place she wanted to be.

She could no more stop blurting the words than she could stop the tidal wave of love that swept through her, giving the words their freedom.

"I love you," she whispered and dropped a kiss on his

bare chest, before nestling her head on his shoulder and falling asleep.

MORNING DAWNED BRIGHT and clear. Karina woke slowly, her body still warm and achy from the night's activities. She bolted upright as memories flooded back. *Brian.* She'd had the most wonderful night of her life. She grinned and bounded out of bed.

Wrapping herself in the sheet, she walked out to the communal room, grateful that Brian's roomies had already left. *Empty.* She stood in the middle of the room, dread forming a sinking ball of steel in her stomach. An engine started outside.

She raced over to the glass doors, stepping out onto the small verandah in time to see Brian's car disappearing down the drive at a good clip. *He was coming back, wasn't he?* She stood there, waiting, for a long time after his car disappeared from view. As her heart broke into a dozen tiny pieces, hope faded away. The small sedan was gone.

And he hadn't once looked back.

TO BE CONTINUED...

Touched by Death

Adult RS/thriller

Death had touched anthropologist Jade Hansen in Haiti once before, costing her an unborn child and perhaps her very sanity.

A year later, determined to face her own issues, she returns to Haiti with a mortuary team to recover the bodies of an American family from a mass grave. Visiting his brother after the quake, independent contractor Dane Carter puts his life on hold to help the sleepy town of Jacmel rebuild. But he finds it hard to like his brother's pregnant wife or her family. He wants to go home, until he meets Jade – and realizes what's missing in his own life. When the mortuary team begins work, it's as if malevolence has been released from the earth. Instead of laying her ghosts to rest, Jade finds herself confronting death and terror again.

And the man who unexpectedly awakens her heart – is right in the middle of it all.

This book is available. Sample chapter is next…

Touched by Death Sample

Prologue

IN PERFECT SYMPHONY the clouds swayed in the sky, wrapping the moon in protective cotton wool as the ground shook and trembled beneath the sleepy town of Jacmel in the south of Haiti.

Mother Earth growled and raged over and over again as if she knew the secrets long kept hidden in the hills behind the small town. As if she knew about the injustices done. As if she knew this had to stop. She gave one last mighty shove and the earth cracked open.

Trees toppled, their roots ripped from the ground in hapless destruction. Large rocks tumbled as their foundations were wiped out from below. Everything fell to the force of Mother Nature – at long last exposing old secrets to the light.

When she was finally satisfied, the clouds slipped back from their protective stance, letting the moon glare upon the result of Mother Earth's game of fifty-two pickup with the Devil. The rays shone on bones long picked clean – now newly exposed to the sky.

The ground undulated one last time. The surrounding hillside shuddered, sending a light dusting of earth and rock to rebury the gruesome evidence. As if the sins of man were too much for even the moon to see.

FIVE DAYS LATER, a tractor, hastily called into service, with a bucket on the front, groaned as it carried yet another load of the town's dead to a large grave. Herman, the tractor driver, was beyond pain and grief and death. He focused on the gritty details of plain survival. Five days of heat and exposure hadn't been kind to the dead – or to the living. Survival had become a grim business and rotting bodies needed to be buried or disease would crush them further. So many dead. No money. No time. No help.

No choice.

His neighbor, John, lifted the last small corpse from the dump truck load on the ground to the loader's bucket. He pulled off one work glove, straightened the bandana tied around his mouth and nose and shouted, "Good to go!"

Herman popped the gear shift forward, swore and prayed that Bertha would survive the job given her. He trundled forward. "Come on girl." He patted the stick shift in his hand. "I need you to get it done. If you quit on me, I ain't gonna make it through this." And that was no joke. He knew for damn sure that he wouldn't if ol' Bertha didn't. *Bad business this.* He had respect for the dead. Every one of his family and friends had received a proper send off, a decent burial – as was fitting. Until this earthquake.

Pain clutched his heart and squeezed. So many dead.

He'd lost his wife, one son and two grandkids this last week. Sex and age hadn't mattered here. Mother Nature hadn't cared. She'd wiped them all out.

John, the only other person who'd stepped up to help, had been lucky. His young wife and her family had survived the devastation. Living out of town had helped. That also contributed to his motivation to help out. This grave butted against his wife's family's land so it made sense for John to make sure this grave was closed over right and proper. There could be many people trekking to the grave on All Soul's Day, as families came to honor their dead. Then again, complete families had been buried together. There might not be anyone left to mourn.

He would come and visit. There were too many people here to forget.

Herman tugged at the old t-shirt tied around his nose and mouth, his black skin blending with the poor light. Nothing kept the smell out. He'd already gone through a half dozen pairs of gloves. But without the makeshift bandana the breath caught in his chest, making him gag. His clothes would have to be burned after this. There would be no way to clean them.

Bertha struggled forward. Darkness hid the evidence of what they were doing. What he'd done. He only hoped he wouldn't have too many more loads to haul.

In the aftermath of the earthquake, everyone had been numb, in shock or frozen with grief. No one had been able to make decisions. There'd been no army to take care of the problem. The government buildings and staff had been as decimated as the rest of the population.

Herman hadn't been able to leave his people lying exposed like that. Determined to do what he could he'd taken command and had done something. Something so awful, he couldn't close his eyes without seeing the stares of the dead – blaming him.

So far, close to sixty people had gone into this pit. The natural depression, a ready-made burial spot, was a godsend to the desperate survivors, a fast answer to the bloated dead rotting on the sidewalks. He didn't know how many more were to come, maybe hundreds. Later, much later, if someone cared, they could open this mass grave and do the right thing. But not now. Now they had to get on with the business of survival.

Mother Nature was a bitch.

Chapter 1

One year later…

JADE HANSEN TWISTED in the cool sheets. Her sweaty panicked body searched for a way out of the endless nightmare of bloated bodies, desperate people and cries for help – pleas that would never get answered. She turned in the fog as one more person, caught among the fallen rocks, cried out to her. She came face to face with a woman – blood congealed in her hair and streaked down the side of her face, a chunk of concrete crushing her legs. She begged for Jade to find her son.

Screaming, Jade took off to the safety of the tent, the tent filled with the dead…and the living that searched for their families.

She couldn't help them all.

She couldn't help any of them.

She couldn't even help herself.

With tears streaming down her face, Jade woke in a panic as if the demons of her nightmare had followed her into the present.

Shuddering, she recognized the hanging lamp overhead as the one in her apartment. The Aztec print couch she'd fallen asleep on was hers, a gift from her brother. And she finally understood that the evening's in-depth television coverage of a small earthquake in Haiti had been the trigger for her nightmare.

Jade curled into a ball, pulling her throw higher up on her neck. She winced at the images still flashing on the news. Another earthquake in Haiti. Only a little one this time. Not that the size mattered. The memories of her one and only humanitarian trip to that area, after the major earthquake almost a year ago, had etched themselves permanently into her brain. A horrible time, a-praying-on-your-knees-for-help kind of horrible time. In Haiti, nightmares had destroyed her sleep. The shortage of food for those suffering had destroyed her appetite.

She'd lost weight over there, but nothing compared to the pounds that had slipped off after her return home. Sure, that had been almost a year ago. It didn't matter. With the nightmare fresh in her mind it felt like only two days.

So much pain and suffering. *So much torment.* She couldn't stop it. She couldn't even begin to make it right. There'd been nothing she could do to help – or so little relative to the scope of the problem, it might as well have been nothing. If she'd been offered a ride out of that hell on any given day, she'd have jumped over her colleagues to grab it.

She wasn't proud of that.

In fact, it made her feel small and ashamed. Her colleagues had done so much better.

She'd wanted to be better. She'd tried to be better.

She'd failed. Failed her colleagues. The victims. And herself.

The memories still haunted her.

She had her nice safe lab job back in Seattle. She drove to work every day in a nice car and returned home every night to her clean safe apartment with running water, heat and electricity. All the comforts denied the Haitians still struggling through the devastation.

After she'd locked her front door behind her that first day home, the tears had started to pour. It seemed she'd been crying ever since.

Her life had gone from bad to worse for a while before she'd picked up – somewhat.

And now another earthquake.

If a small one like that triggered her memories what was the reality doing to all those poor people still living the horror?

The phone rang.

She ignored it.

It wouldn't quit. Finally, she couldn't stand it so picked up the receiver. She didn't even bother to check the caller ID. Duncan called every night at nine.

"I'm fine, Duncan."

"Hey, Kitten." Her brother's pet name for her made her smile as he'd probably intended. She used to be like him. Upbeat, funny and carefree. Until life had dumped her on her ass at the top of the slide and given her a hard kick downhill. She wasn't sure she'd hit bottom now either.

"I've got a job proposition for you."

His cheerful voice made her want to smile. The job proposition didn't. "I don't want to hear it."

He laughed, a buoyant sound that rang around the room. He never failed to raise her spirits. The effect just didn't hang around after his calls. "Maybe you don't, but maybe you do. How will you know if you don't hear it? It's a good one."

His wheedling tone made her smile in spite of her horrible mood. "Not if I don't want to hear it."

"You don't know what you want."

Jade groaned. "If I don't know, then how do you?"

That laughter pealed again. She shook her head and felt the lightness – the joyful spirit that was her brother – ease the ache in her soul. "I know you keep trying to save me, Duncan, but I'm fine."

The laughter and joy cut off suddenly. Duncan's voice, sober and sad, whispered, "No. No, you're not."

Tears choked her. She rubbed her eyes. She wasn't going to cry, damn it. Not tonight. Not *again* tonight.

"This has to stop, Jade. You're going to collapse and I don't want that to happen." Love slipped through the phone receiver making it harder to hold back the tears. Jade didn't trust herself to speak. She sniffled ever so slightly.

"I know you're hurting inside. I feel it and I hurt for you."

"I know," she whispered, starting to shake, knowing she had to stop – only she didn't know how. And once again – couldn't deal with it. "Look, I'm really tired. I need to get to bed. I'll talk to you tomorrow."

She didn't give him a chance to say good-bye and hung up instead. As soon as the receiver clicked down, the tears rolled. Hot and steady, they streamed down her cheeks. She snuggled back into the couch and let them run.

The point of stopping them was long gone – besides she no longer knew how.

"HEY DANE. THAT guy called again." John called out.

"Yeah, which guy?" Dane walked over to stand beside his stepbrother who'd stopped by the site for a visit.

Dane tugged his hard hat off to wipe the sweat running

down his forehead. Christ it was hot and humid here. He surveyed the hospital construction site in front of them. Not bad at all. They were ahead of schedule, but completion of the new wing was still months away. Jacmel hadn't recovered from the last big earthquake and with smaller ones continually causing setbacks, the country would be years getting back on its feet.

It had taken weeks to convince John to let him come over after the quake. When he'd realized how badly in need the town was, Dane had stepped in. But John had refused Dane's help to fix John's small engine repair shop that had been decimated in one of the smaller more recent earthquakes. John said he wanted to fix things himself.

"The guy about the grave." John said, "Remember they want to open it and retrieve some guy's family?"

Dane glanced over at his brother. There were only the two of them left in the family. Both stubborn. Independent. And family oriented. It had only taken one phone call with something odd in John's voice to catch Dane's attention. He'd put his Seattle construction business in the hands of his capable foreman, an old school friend, and without his brother's invite, he'd flown to Haiti two days later. That had been months ago.

Shielding his eyes from the hot sun, Dane said, "I have to admit, never-ending sunshine and warm, dry weather is hardly a hardship. Of course we haven't hit the humid summer season, yet."

"See? Isn't this much better than the wet misery of the coast? Seattle is probably still buried in snow – even in March." John grinned with satisfaction.

Dane couldn't argue that. His foreman had been complaining of just that in the last phone call. "Not everyone hates the rain like you do."

"Come on, admit it." John reached over and smacked Dane's shoulder. A cloud of dust rose, making him step back hurriedly. "You love it here."

"I love visiting you and of course, I adore Tasha." Dane grinned over his white lie. There was no arguing that Tasha obviously adored his brother so that was good enough for him. It had, after all, been the call of family that had brought Dane here.

John had a terrible history with relationships. His long-time high school sweetheart had walked out the door of her home one day just weeks before graduation and had never returned. A few years later, John had married the witchy Elise. That marriage had been a walking disaster right from the wedding reception. Dane hadn't been able to stand the woman and the feeling had been mutual. John was just a big teddy bear who attracted unscrupulous people.

After that fiasco, John disappeared for years before finally setting up housekeeping with Tasha in Haiti. Dane's antennae went off at that and given the past, he could be forgiven for worrying about his brother. Only John appeared to have stabilized, was flourishing even. Dane had been delighted.

The major earthquake had changed all that, sending John back into the same morose angry man as before.

"Hey, are you in there?"

Dane started.

John smirked at him, a sign his light-hearted kid brother was showing through the more cynical angry one of recent years. "What's the matter; Felice getting to you?"

Heat washed over Dane's throat. Felice was too hot, too willing and way too young. She was also the daughter of one of Tasha's friends who'd visited yesterday. He didn't know the specific laws in Haiti relating to that sort of thing, still he was pretty damn sure he'd get jail time back home and that was deterrent enough for him.

"She needs to be locked away for a few years."

"Not here. Girls her age are often married and pregnant." John added thoughtfully, "And not likely in that order."

Dane shook his head. "As long as it's not to me."

John changed the subject abruptly. "What am I going to do about the call…about this guy's request for help at the mass gravesite? Sounds crazy to me."

Easily following the lightning shift of his brother's mind, Dane said, "What's to do – he's a grieving man. His request isn't unreasonable. And it's done all the time."

John visibly shuddered. "I never expected to feel so strongly about it, but after that earthquake… I don't know Dane. I saw too much death. More than I should have – more than anyone should have. It seems wrong to dig up those poor earthquake victims again."

"You've been living here too long. Some weird Haitian's beliefs are rubbing off on you."

John snickered, making Dane laugh. "Or not long enough. According to Tasha, Mother Earth claimed them and she won't be happy if she's forced to give them up again."

With a sigh of disgust, Dane said, "That's crazy talk. This guy lost his family. He wants to take the three of them home to Seattle and bury them properly. He needs closure. That's all. What's so wrong about that?"

John kicked a stray rock in the dirt. "I don't know that anything is wrong with it. I guess if it were me and mine, I'd want to take them home, too. But it's a mass grave. There are other bodies to consider. Other families who will be hurt."

"Really?" Dane stared at him. "Like *how mass?*"

John shot him a look before grimacing and staring off in the horizon. "I stopped counting at sixty. We did what we had to do. The dead…they were everywhere. Herman, our old neighbor, used his loader…Christ it was bad."

Dane scrunched his face. John rushed to explain.

"God, there were children playing beside bloated bodies. They'd become dulled to them; there were so many. Oh don't blame the children. They stayed close to the people they knew because they had no one else. That a dead mother or sibling lay within a few feet didn't seem to matter. Even dead, they were a comfort."

Dane closed his eyes as terrible images flooded his mind. He couldn't imagine the horror. "I wasn't judging. I just can't envision what you went through. And to think of children sitting there, so lost and alone… Well…it's a terrible thought."

Shadows darkened John's eyes. Dane was sorry for what John had been through. "That's the thing about family." Dane patted John on the shoulder and noticed his brother cringe.

"So you think this guy should be allowed to come in and remove his kin?" John wasn't backing away from this one.

"I don't have any say in this. I wasn't aware that you did, either. I'm sure this man has already gone through the authorities. I'd suggest that you accept that this is going to happen whether you want it to or not. The team of specialists is going to be here soon. When they arrive, be nice to them. Helpful. They will probably be there for a day or two, a week or two max. Then they'll be gone, leaving the others to rest in peace."

"It's not that easy."

"I know. There are other people with loved ones in that grave. Maybe someone should suggest that all the victims be identified and even…" Dane pursed his lips and nodded his head, pleased with his idea. "Reburied properly. This guy has money. Maybe some of it should be put toward assisting the community to help them deal with disaster."

John shook his head. "You don't understand the full scope of the problem here. There could be hundreds of bodies there. We just kept putting them in then piling dirt and rocks on top to make sure they weren't disturbed. We probably went overboard on that part."

Dane blanched. "Hundreds?" He swallowed heavily. "Okay so maybe the team will need a little longer. Still something could be done for the other remains." Dane winced. "Or at least the remains they can find and identify while they search for the ones they are shipping back to Seattle."

John stared at him, and gulped. "That's not helping."

"Yeah. I know. Sorry about that."

The two men stared at the half-completed building in front of them. Dane took an involuntary step back. Right now the damn thing resembled a skeleton reaching out of the ground.

TO BE CONTINUED…

Tuesday's Child

What she doesn't want…is exactly what he needs.

Shunned and ridiculed all her life for something she can't control, Samantha Blair hides her psychic abilities and lives on the fringes of society. Against her will, however, she's tapped into a killer – or rather, his victims. Each woman's murder, blow-by-blow, ravages her mind until their death releases her back to her body. Sam knows she must go to the authorities, but will the rugged, no-nonsense detective in charge of tracking down the killer believe her?

Detective Brandt Sutherland only trusts hard evidence, yet Sam's visions offer clues he needs to catch a killer. The more he learns about her incredible abilities, however, the clearer it becomes that Sam's visions have put her in the killer's line of fire. Now Brandt must save her from something he cannot see or understand…and risk losing his heart in the process.

As danger and desire collide, passion raises the stakes in a game Sam and Brandt don't dare lose.

Broken Protocols

Romantic comedy & suspense

Dani's been through a year of hell…

Just as it's getting better, she's tossed forward through time with her orange Persian cat, Charmin Marvin, clutched in her arms. They're dropped into a few centuries into the future. There's nothing she can do to stop it, and it's impossible to go back.

And then it gets worse…

A year of government regulation is easing, and Levi Blackburn is feeling back in control. If he can keep his reckless brother in check, everything will be perfect. But while he's been protecting Milo from the government, Milo's been busy working on a present for him…

The present is Dani, only she comes with a snarky cat who suddenly starts talking…and doesn't know when to shut up.

In an age where breaking protocols have severe consequences, things go wrong, putting them all in danger…

It's a Dog's Life

Romantic comedy & suspense

It's the first day of Ninna's job in the local animal shelter…and a dog is talking to her. Not just any dog…a fat, old, smart-alecky Basset Hound who says his name is Mosey.

She can't quit, she needs this job. And then there's the yummy vet. Who turns out to live across the street from her in a much bigger house than her tiny house. Big enough to hold a few animals – including the mouthy Mosey. With all this going on, she doesn't have time to worry about the rash of break-ins and the sense of being watched. She's too busy worrying that she's nuts.

When Ninna agrees to dog sit for the cute vet from work, she sees it as a trial at being a pet owner and a way to build on her budding relationship with the vet. For Mosey, this weekend means time to get to know each other.

For the stalker who's tracking Ninna's movements, it means…opportunity.

About the Author

Dale Mayer is a *USA Today* best-selling author, best known for her SEALs military romances, her Psychic Visions series, and her Lovely Lethal Garden cozy series. Her contemporary romances are raw and full of passion and emotion (Broken But ... Mending, Hathaway House series). Her thrillers will keep you guessing (Kate Morgan, By Death series), and her romantic comedies will keep you giggling (*It's a Dog's Life*, a stand-alone novella; and the Broken Protocols series, starring Charming Marvin, the cat).

Dale honors the stories that come to her—and some of them are crazy, break all the rules and cross multiple genres!

To go with her fiction, she also writes nonfiction in many different fields, with books available on résumé writing, companion gardening, and the US mortgage system. All her books are available in print and ebook format.

Connect with Dale Mayer Online

Dale's Website – www.dalemayer.com
Twitter – @DaleMayer
Facebook Page – geni.us/DaleMayerFBFanPage
Facebook Group – geni.us/DaleMayerFBGroup
BookBub – geni.us/DaleMayerBookbub
Instagram – geni.us/DaleMayerInstagram
Goodreads – geni.us/DaleMayerGoodreads
Newsletter – geni.us/DaleNews

Also by Dale Mayer

Published Adult Books:

Psychic Vision Series

Tuesday's Child

Hide'n Go Seek

Maddy's Floor

Garden of Sorrow

Knock, Knock...

Rare Find

Eyes to the Soul

Now You See Her

Shattered

Into the Abyss

Psychic Visions Books 1–3

Psychic Visions Books 4–6

Psychic Visions Books 7–9

By Death Series

Touched by Death – Part 1

Touched by Death – Part 2

Touched by Death – Parts 1&2

Haunted by Death

Chilled by Death

By Death Books 1–3

Second Chances...at Love Series

Second Chances – Part 1

Second Chances – Part 2

Second Chances – complete book (Parts 1 & 2)

Charmin Marvin Romantic Comedy Series

Broken Protocols

Broken Protocols 2

Broken Protocols 3

Broken Protocols 3.5

Broken Protocols 1-3

Broken and... Mending

Skin

Scars

Scales (of Justice)

Broken but... Mending 1-3

Glory

Genesis

Tori

Celeste

Glory Trilogy

Biker Blues

Biker Blues: Morgan, Part 1

Biker Blues: Morgan, Part 2

Biker Blues: Morgan, Part 3

Biker Baby Blues: Morgan, Part 4

Biker Blues: Morgan, Full Set

Biker Blues: Salvation, Part 1

Biker Blues: Salvation, Part 2

Biker Blues: Salvation, Part 3

Biker Blues: Salvation, Full Set

SEALs of Honor

Mason: SEALs of Honor, Book 1

Hawk: SEALs of Honor, Book 2

Dane: SEALs of Honor, Book 3

Swede: SEALs of Honor, Book 4

Shadow: SEALs of Honor, Book 5

Cooper: SEALs of Honor, Book 6

Markus: SEALs of Honor, Book 7

Evan: SEALs of Honor, Book 8

Mason's Wish: SEALs of Honor, Book 9

SEALs of Honor, Books 1–3

SEALs of Honor, Books 4–6

Collections

Dare to Be You…

Dare to Love…

Dare to be Strong…

RomanceX3

Standalone Novellas

It's a Dog's Life

Riana's Revenge

Published Young Adult Books:

Family Blood Ties Series

Vampire in Denial

Vampire in Distress

Vampire in Design

Vampire in Deceit

Vampire in Defiance

Vampire in Conflict

Vampire in Chaos

Vampire in Crisis

Vampire in Control

Vampire in Charge

Family Blood Ties Set 1–3

Family Blood Ties Set 1–5

Family Blood Ties Set 4–6

Family Blood Ties Set 7–9

Sian's Solution – A Family Blood Ties Short Story

Design series

Dangerous Designs

Deadly Designs

Darkest Designs

Design Series Trilogy

Standalone

In Cassie's Corner

Gem Stone (a Gemma Stone Mystery)

Time Thieves

Published Non-Fiction Books:

Career Essentials

Career Essentials: The Résumé

Career Essentials: The Cover Letter

Career Essentials: The Interview

Career Essentials: 3 in 1